To Tame a Wolf

by

JoAnn Black

This is a work of fiction. Names, characters, places, and incidents are either the product of the author's imagination or are used fictitiously, and any resemblance to actual persons living or dead, business establishments, events, or locales, is entirely coincidental.

To Tame a Wolf

Cover Art by *Diana Carlile*

The Wild Rose Press, Inc.
PO Box 708
Adams Basin, NY 14410-0708
Visit us at www.thewildrosepress.com

Publishing History
First Tea Rose Edition, 2017
Print ISBN 978-1-5092-1619-2
Digital ISBN 978-1-5092-1620-8

Published in the United States of America

The McGregor glared as he strode back.
She lifted her chin and glared right back at him. When he got close enough to reach her, his hands snaked out, and he grabbed her upper arms and pulled her abruptly against his chest. Startled, she looked up at him with her mouth open to protest. He brought his face down within inches of hers and said in a whisper, "The next time I tell you to do something"—and the whisper escalated to a roar—"by God, you better do it!" He gave her an extra little shake, before pushing her away.

Stunned, she yelled back, "You're mad at me? I came back to help you, you idiot!"

The McGregor pounded his massive chest with a fist, emphasizing each syllable as he yelled, "Do. I. Look. Like. I. Need. Help? Especially from a woman?"

Alexandra stared up into his angry face. *Actually, no, he didn't look like he needed anyone's assistance. He looked like a giant, a fierce warrior.* She took a deep breath and talked calmly to ease the building tension between them, "You may not have needed my help, but I *did* help. Next time, I'll leave you to your own devices."

"What you *did*, was almost get me killed!" He glanced down at his bleeding arm.

Alexandra hadn't noticed until then. Blood dripped from the fingertips of his left hand. She gasped and stated the obvious, "You're injured!"

Dedication

Dedicated to my sister and sister-in-law,
both of whom died of cancer
during the writing of this book.
Their courage will never be forgotten.

Chapter One

Alexandra knelt before the altar. The uneven edges of the stone floor dug into her knees. Ignoring the pain, she prayed. "Please God, don't make me go back. Save me, intervene on my behalf." She trembled from both cold and fear. There was no heat source in the sanctuary except from the candles she'd lit. Finally, when she could no longer endure the pain, she rose and paced from one side of the sanctuary to the other. She looked at how far the candles had burned down and knew that little time remained. The night had passed far too quickly. Stopping in front of the altar, she knelt once more, grimacing when her bruised knees met the floor. Tears ran down her face as she implored, "Lord, if I must go, make me strong, make me brave, give me wisdom—"

The heavy sanctuary door squeaked open, and the clicking of approaching footsteps interrupted her plea.

"Alexandra, they have come!" an anxious voice whispered.

Finishing the prayer in silence, she stood and wiped away her tears before turning around to face her friend. The novice nun stood before her wringing her hands. Alexandra smiled in reassurance and gave her friend a warm hug.

"I shall miss you so much!"

"You will be in all our prayers," the young nun

said, holding back her tears.

"Come, let's not keep them waiting. They are probably most anxious to depart."

****

There were at least twenty men in the guard sent to collect her, and as Alexandra scanned their faces, none looked familiar. Armor clad and sitting on their mounts, the men openly stared with interest and curiosity while she said her goodbyes to the group of habit-clad women huddled together in front of the abbey. Each woman gave her a hug, a word of advice, or a small parting gift. Alexandra dearly loved each and every one of them. They had raised her into adulthood, and as mentors, each had contributed in some way to the woman she had become. She resolved never, ever to forget them.

Turning back to the guard, she waited until a horse was brought forward and her meager bags secured to it. The dawn was cold, and as the horses stomped impatiently, their breath hung in the air as wisps of clouds. The men remained quiet, with only the creaking of leather and the occasional clank of armor filling the silence. The closest guardsman assisted her in mounting the large, white mare. A fur cloak was thrown over her shoulders, and an older man, who had introduced himself as captain of the guard, motioned the party forward. Alexandra turned back to wave and to lock into her memory the place that had been her home for the last seven years.

How fitting, she thought wryly, that it was a cold, dreary day in which she rode back to hell. Why had her cousin, Niles Conrad, summoned her after all these years? It couldn't be good. Not good at all. The last time she'd seen the man, he'd almost beaten her to death.

Afterward, Niles had ordered her unconscious body be removed from the estate in the middle of the night, and she had been delivered to the abbey the following day. With the nuns' expertise and tender care, her broken bones mended, and her open wounds healed with little scarring. With every step her horse took, memories came flooding back. Memories she'd left buried a long time.

Her horse slid on an incline of mud. She clutched the pommel tightly and shifted her weight to remain seated. Riding side-saddle was no easy feat. Her father used to let her ride astride like a boy whenever they rode together around the estate.

Paying more attention to her horse and its path, Alexandra took in the countryside. A patchwork of snow, ice, and mud covered the rolling hills. Where the sun landed, the top soil was slippery, but in shade, there was ice. How she longed for colorful flowers and green meadow grass! Winter had been long and harsh, and it was not over yet.

Riding among so many men, Alexandra felt shy and uncomfortable. It had been a long time since she had even been in the presence of men. She avoided making eye contact and kept her eyes on her horse or the scenery. No matter how she tried to keep her thoughts in check, they kept straying back to Niles.

Alexandra had been on the threshold of womanhood when Niles returned as a man to take over the responsibilities of Ravenwood. She liked him even less than she remembered.

At first, he was just arrogant and pompous, pleased by the turn of events that gave him so much power and control, but it didn't take long for his true colors to show.

Forcing herself to think about more pleasant things, she thought about how good and peaceful life had been at the abbey. She was allowed to study anything she pleased, and what pleased her the most was mastering the art of healing herbs. Sister Francis had passed on her knowledge and encouraged her studies. There was always something new to learn.

Hours passed and the scenery changed little. Were the guards ever going to stop and rest the horses? Her bottom was both sore and numb, and she really needed to relieve herself, but she was too embarrassed to ask them to stop. The cold wasn't helping any. Pulling the cloak tighter, she thought the day seemed colder instead of warmer. Finally, the captain of the guard called the party to a halt when they neared a stream.

The guardsman who had been riding on her right took her horse's reins and held the animal still while she clumsily dismounted. Looking up to meet his eyes for the first time, she said, "Thank you." He nodded and led her horse along with his to the stream.

There wasn't much privacy offered among the leafless trees. Alexandra noted a full pine tree farther in and headed toward it. She didn't hear the growl at first, but instantly froze when it grew louder. Less than ten feet in front of her crouched a large, gray wolf. Fear stuck in her throat, and she was unable to move or make a sound. With lips curled back to show large fangs dripping with saliva, the wolf watched her with piercing eyes and made guttural noises.

Alexandra finally managed to draw in air and ever so slowly stepped back. The wolf, in the same instant, sprang toward her. Time slowed as the wolf hovered in the air before suddenly dropping like a stone at her feet, an arrow protruding from its side. Gasping, she stumbled back and stared in disbelief at the dead animal when members of the guard rushed forward.

"I got him!" a young guardsman exclaimed. He didn't appear much older than she was.

"Good shot, Thomas," she heard, as members of the guard gathered to congratulate the young man and admire the wolf.

"It must weigh at least a hundred pounds," another man stated.

"Odd for a wolf to attack in broad daylight with so many people around," said the captain of the guard and he started to walk around the area.

Her legs trembling, Alexandra stumbled away from the excitement and found a sheltered place to relieve herself. She then sat on a fallen log to gain her composure and to will her limbs to stop shaking. *Thank you, Lord, for keeping me safe.* After several moments, she headed back toward the men and horses.

"Ah ha!" exclaimed the captain, "Look here! This is the reason the she-wolf was so bold." He held up a small, struggling ball of fur by the scruff of its neck. The animal started yipping and growling. The captain withdrew a dagger from his belt.

"No!" Alexandra yelled. "Please don't hurt it!" She ran over to the captain's side. Taking the fraught animal, she held it against her chest. Its little heart thundered against hers.

"My lady, the pup will not survive without his mother. Killing him swiftly is the humane thing to do."

"There's no need. I'll take care of him."

"You can't seriously think of taking that little beast with us!" The captain sheathed his weapon and put his hands on his hips.

Looking the captain straight in the eye, she said, "I'll not be leaving without him." She could see the man scheming in his head. "I'll fight you if you try to take him from me. How would it look to my cousin Niles if you delivered me all bloody and bruised? And with my clothing torn and disheveled?" The men looked at one another.

"Fine," the captain mumbled gruffly, "but I'll be leaving it to you to explain it to him."

****

Back on the trail again with the young, male wolf pup tucked under her cloak against her body, Alexandra felt better than she had since they started this journey. It helped to have something else to think about other than her problems. It was obvious the guard did not know the relationship that existed between her and her cousin. Niles would have laughed and given them a reward or promotion for delivering her in a gruesome state. Alexandra wondered what had happened to members of the old guard. She couldn't blame anyone for not wanting to work for her cousin.

The puppy stopped trembling and grew still. She must try to find something for him to eat and drink the next time they stopped to water the horses. She would have to be very careful when they got to Ravenwood to keep Niles from finding out about the pup, for there was no doubt he would kill it. Her thoughts turned to God. Did He hold her life in His hands, as she held the pup's life in hers? She closed her eyes and prayed. "Lord, help me to trust that You have me in the palm of

Your hand, and that by letting them take me to Niles, You have a plan to keep me safe."

The reins slipped through her fingers. Her eyes opened quickly.

"I'm sorry, my lady. I thought you had fallen asleep," said Thomas, the young guard who had saved her life. "Why don't you let me take the reins? Then you can sleep or tend to the wolf easier."

She smiled wearily and handed them over. "Thank you, and I thank you for saving my life back there." The young man blushed and nodded as he took charge of her horse.

****

Alexandra shivered from the cold and clenched her teeth to keep them from chattering. Every bone in her body ached. The sun had set hours ago, and Thomas told her they would soon be approaching Ravenwood. Each step her horse took brought her closer to her fate. She feared what waited for her and asked God to give her strength to face what lay ahead.

The pup seemed to sense her dismay and grew increasingly restless. She drew his body out from under her cloak and held him in front of her face. His little tongue licked her chin, and she smiled. "What shall I name you, my friend?" she asked, before tucking him away again as it began to rain. The freezing drops cut her to the bone. Her hands and feet were numb.

"I see lights," her riding companion said. "We are almost there, my lady."

"Thomas, may I ask a favor? Will you take the pup and keep him hidden until you can put him in my chambers? And please, don't tell anyone."

"Certainly," the young guard replied, eager to

please. Holding out his hands, he accepted the squirming pup.

Within minutes, they passed through the main gate of the keep. There were appreciative murmurs and groans all around as everyone dismounted at the stable. The captain of the guard commanded that Alexandra's bags be taken to her room. Taking her by the arm, he steered her toward the entrance of her former home.

"Sir Conrad asked that I bring you to the main hall as soon as we arrived," he said.

She steeled herself against facing Niles again. She'd learned it was always best not to show any emotion whatsoever, for he took great pleasure in seeing her fear or pain. Keeping a calm mask on her face, she quoted scripture to herself and allowed the captain to usher her through the torch-lit entryway and into the large, dark hall.

It took several seconds for her eyes to adjust. Only the two large fireplaces at each end of the rectangular room were lit, and they cast dancing shadows upon the rest of the room. The captain announced her arrival, bowed, and left the hall. She stood alone, trembling, and faced the two occupants of the room she could now see sitting at the long, wooden table. Her cousin Niles sat at the head of the table. The flickering shadows crossing his face made him appear even more sinister than usual. He'd gotten fat! Surrounded by food plates and wine, he looked up at her and then pointed with the turkey leg in his hand. He guffawed. "Here's your bride-to-be now!"

Chapter Two

Alexandra held back a gasp and quickly turned to look at her cousin's companion. From where the man sat, she could only see the back of him until he staggered to his feet and turned to face her. He was obviously drunk as he swayed from side to side making his way across the long room toward her. He stopped midway, then began cursing, and kicked at something on the ground. To her dismay, that something seemed to be a man chained to the floor. The crumpled, bloodied mass emitted a slight moan, and the drunkard quit stomping. Appearing satisfied with his captive's reaction, he moved toward her.

He was older than her cousin, probably in his fifties, and food particles clung to his beard. He grinned when he stopped in front of her, and she noticed that he also had several missing teeth. Squinting at her as if trying to focus his beady eyes, he said, "You didn't tell me she was a beauty." Alexandra stiffened as the man reached out and grasped a handful of her long hair.

"Like gold, it is," he murmured, letting the silken strands run through his fingers.

"Huh," Niles replied as if suddenly bored and took another bite. "I think she's rather homely myself."

The stranger's eyes combed her figure, pausing to linger over her ample breasts and small waist.

"Aye, she'll do just fine," he panted. He grabbed

her jaw with rough hands and pried her mouth open, inspecting her teeth.

"Can she talk?" he asked, his sour breath brushing against her face.

Repelled, Alexandra pulled her head from his hands and stepped back. "I can speak," she stated coldly. "Keep your filthy hands to yourself."

The foul man frowned at her words.

"Now, now, is that any way to speak to your betrothed?" Niles smiled. "Your future husband's name is Hugh Sullivan, and you'll be married just as soon as Hugh and I can come to terms on our agreement." Gloating at her dismay, he said, "You see my dear, once you're married, Hugh and I will split your estate, and together we will join forces to defeat Hugh's enemy, the McGregor, and then we'll split his lands too."

At the mention of the name McGregor, the man named Hugh grumbled and swayed his way back toward the unconscious body on the floor. Alexandra had momentarily forgotten that he was there. She heard another muffled moan as Hugh kicked him several more times. Her heart went out to him. The poor man's face was a mess. His eyes were swollen, and his nose looked broken. Dried, caked blood covered his face. He was also covered in mud and filth, but she could still see that he wore the McGregor colors.

Knowing from experience that interfering with the poor man's torture would only make things worse for him, Alexandra drew their attention back to herself by saying, "You can't force me to marry anyone against my will."

"Oh really, and who's going to stop me?" Niles

sneered. "The priest? He has his price." Wiping his mouth on his sleeve and pouring himself more wine, he suggested, "Perhaps Hugh would like a trial sample of his future wife's affections?"

"Aye!" Hugh agreed, eyeing her eagerly.

Alexandra hid her repulsion behind a stoic expression.

"On second thought, let's not be too hasty, Hugh," Niles said. "You may decide you don't like the taste of her, and then where would I be?"

"Aggie!!" Niles bellowed for his housekeeper. A few seconds later an old woman appeared. "Bring us more wine, and escort *her*"—nodding toward Alexandra—"to her rooms and lock her in."

The gray-haired Aggie looked up at Alexandra with dawning recognition and then spat in her direction. "What's she doing back here?" She glared with contempt at the girl.

Niles chuckled. He had always enjoyed the old crone's attitude toward her. "Don't worry. She won't be staying long, and don't trouble yourself getting her anything to eat. I'm sure she had plenty on the journey," he added while filling his plate with more food.

Hugh's gaze never left Alexandra as she followed the old woman from the room.

"Come my friend, let us drink and make plans," she heard Niles say before the door shut behind her.

****

Alexandra silently followed the woman through the halls. She was pleased to see she was being led in the direction of her old rooms. Neither she nor the woman spoke to the servants they encountered on the way.

11

Alexandra couldn't help but notice how her home had deteriorated during her absence. Art pieces no longer adorned the walls. The plush window coverings and silver candle holders were also missing.

Upon approaching her bedroom door, the old woman pulled a bracelet of keys from her apron pocket and unlocked it. She did not step back for Alexandra to enter but entered the room herself. Alexandra followed and promptly shut the door. The two women stood and stared at one another for a second before quietly squealing and throwing their arms around each other.

The old woman pulled back first and framed Alexandra's face in her hands. "Look at you, my child," she exclaimed with tears in her eyes, "You're all grown up! You remind me of your mother."

"Oh Aggie, I didn't think I'd ever see you again!" Alexandra exclaimed and gave the older woman another hug. It had been Aggie who came up with the idea of portraying the image of disliking one another, as loyal servants were being let go at the time. The old woman was a great actress, and she embellished her role. She was also quite the Scotswoman with no love for the English. Although Alexandra was English, Aggie had known and helped care for her since her birth, and she had been a great comfort to Alexandra since her parents' deaths.

"I'd better go take the peacock his wine before he starts wondering where I am. I'll be back as soon as I can. We've plans to make," Aggie said with a wink before slipping out the door.

Alexandra looked around her chambers. Apparently, Aggie had heard word that she'd been sent for. Nostalgia hit her as she remembered the room from her childhood. The chamber was spotlessly clean, and a fire blazed in the hearth. Her traveling bags leaned against the wall in one corner of the room.

Hearing a soft whine, Alexandra opened the door to her dressing room. There in the middle of the floor was a timber box which held her furry new friend. His coat was a mixture of gray and white, and only his front paws and nose could be seen above the top edge. He must have sensed her presence as he started yipping with excitement. Alexandra darted across to pick him up. As remote as her rooms were from the rest of the keep, she doubted that anyone could really hear his cries, but she didn't want to take any chances. He wriggled happily against her, licking her face whenever he got the chance. She would have to tell Aggie about him and ask her for some milk or meat.

Thomas had placed a woolen blanket in the bottom of the box, as well as a stone cup full of water. The structure was big enough for the pup to take care of his business at the other end. Thomas had done a good job. She was grateful.

Alexandra carried the cub as she paced about her chambers. What was she to do? She would rather die than marry that disgusting creature downstairs. If she escaped and ran back to the abbey, that would undoubtedly be the first place Niles would look, and she didn't want to put her friends there in any danger. She paced back and forth as she thought. The door opened, and Aggie appeared. She came in carrying two bowls of porridge.

"One for the pup," she said, and set the bowl upon the floor near the hearth. "I caught your young man sneaking him in when they dropped off your bags. After scaring the daylights out of him, I extracted his promise of secrecy."

Alexandra put the pup down next to the bowl and dipped her finger into it and then wiped her finger on the pup's tongue. He was so hungry that it didn't take him long to get the idea and soon he started licking from the bowl.

"Thank you," Alexandra said, and she gestured for Aggie to sit in the lone chair by the fire before sitting at her feet.

"Aggie, what am I to do? I have to leave. Did you hear Niles's plans for me? And why is there a McGregor man chained to the floor?" The questions came pouring from her.

"I've listened to the two of them scheming for weeks. Hugh Sullivan has a reputation for being almost as bad as your cousin. Yesterday, a Sullivan hunting party came across this lone McGregor near the Sullivan-McGregor border. They say that he killed half the hunting party before he was captured. The Sullivan brought him here to keep the McGregor clan from attacking the Sullivans, should word of the abduction leak out. They want to find a weakness in the McGregor clan's defenses that might aid their attack. However, this McGregor clansman is surprisingly strong, and they've not gotten a word out of him. I fear they'll end up killing him before he speaks."

Both women were quiet as they thought. The pup had finished his supper and in his attempt to lick the bowl clean, he was chasing it across the floor as it scooted out from under him.

"I don't remember much about the McGregors except for the name. What can you tell me about them?" Alexandra asked.

"Well, they be a fierce fighting clan. They tend to keep to themselves most times. The old McGregor died several years back, and now one of his sons, a man they call the Wolf has become clan leader. He is called such because of his reputation for being cunning and ferocious in battle. I have a niece who married into the clan, but I haven't spoken to her in years," Aggie replied.

Alexandra stood up and started pacing once again. *Lord, is this a coincidence? I rescue a wolf pup and hours later learn of this leader named Wolf? Or is it a sign from you?* As a plan began to bloom in her mind, Alexandra grabbed Aggie's hand and said, "Aggie, do you think I could get this McGregor to take me to his laird? In exchange for his freedom? I could warn the laird of Niles's plans, and perhaps he will grant me shelter. If nothing else, it would buy me time."

"You would have to steal the man out from under their noses." Aggie stood. "I don't see how that would be possible."

Alexandra continued to pace. After a few minutes, she said, "I think I know how it can be done. I have learned much about medicine in the years I've been gone, and I have many supplies with me in my bags. We could add a sleeping powder to their wine. It would be risky. They may be able to taste the bitterness."

"Aye," Aggie agreed, "it could work. They are so deep into their cups now that they probably won't even notice, and if they do, I could say that the bottle must not be properly fermented yet, and must have gotten mixed in with the older bottles by mistake. How long before this potion would take effect?"

"It should take no more than fifteen or twenty minutes if they drink the whole bottle, and they will wake up with terrific hangovers. Hopefully, they will just believe they passed out from drinking too much. Can you pull it off, Aggie? I don't want to put you in danger."

"Aye, my part will be easy," she replied. "You, on the other hand, will have to take a barely conscious, injured man through rough terrain in the middle of the night, and you have a two or three day journey ahead of you, if they don't catch up to you first."

"Believe me, it is much better than the alternative," Alexandra said. "And if we cannot rouse this man, I will attempt to go on my own even though I don't know if I can find the way."

Aggie replied, "Follow the creek to the northwest corner of your property. You know the way. That will probably take you the rest of what's left of the night. Continue north. Hopefully, the McGregor will be alert enough to help you by then." She held out her hand. "Give me that powder now. Niles should be asking for another bottle soon, if they are not already passed out. If we are to do this, it must be done with haste."

As soon as Aggie left the room, Alexandra started packing the essentials she would need, which included all her medicinal herbs as well as a change of clothing. She knew it was foolish, but she didn't want to leave the pup behind. Aggie was kept too busy by Niles to have enough time to care for it, and she didn't really trust anyone else with the task. Besides, she felt that her fate and the fate of the cub were somehow entwined. From a wool blanket, she created a sling she could put over her head. The sling would work much like those that carried human babies, and she could wear it under her cloak.

Aggie re-appeared at the door. She was carrying a satchel and a fur cloak. "Good timing," she said. "They were almost finished with the last bottle, and they were too drunk to notice any difference in taste. I went to the stables after and told Lem to saddle two horses. He will have them for you at the creek." Lem had been Aggie's sweetheart for as long as Alexandra could remember. "As long as you don't make too much noise, you should be able to get to them without any trouble." She lifted the satchel. "I have packed food and supplies, and I have taken Niles's best cloak for the McGregor."

"I'd be lost without you, Aggie," Alexandra declared. "Now if we can only get the McGregor up and moving."

****

Ian McGregor lay still on the floor while contemplating his dilemma. He'd been an idiot for not listening to his brother regarding taking men with him on his hunt, but the clan was not currently at war since the last feud with the Campbells. Ian had wanted time for himself away from everyone, and he'd been yearning for the peace and quiet of the forest. Apparently, he was wrong about not having any current enemies.

It was indeed fortunate for him that he had not been recognized as the McGregor laird. His head pounded and his ribs hurt with every breath he took. He hadn't heard their voices for a while, and he hoped they were passed out. Slowly sitting up, he bit back an oath as pain stabbed through him and the room spun. He could barely see out of a slit in his right eye. Yes, both bastards were passed out.

He quietly pulled on his chains. His wrists had been chained as well as his legs, and the leg chain was anchored to a loop in the floor. There was no give in the loop, not that he expected any. Tomorrow morning, before they started to work on him in earnest, he would attempt to take one of them. He was not as badly off as he pretended to be. He had played at being unconscious several times, and he made sure to moan with every kick and blow. The next time he feigned sleep and the Sullivan came close enough to kick him again, Ian intended to sweep Sullivan's feet out from under him and crush the pig's head between his thighs. He might not be able to escape, but he would take as many men down with him as he could before he was killed.

Ian stiffened when he heard soft footsteps approaching the hall. He lay back down, feigning sleep.

****

Alexandra cautiously approached the hall entrance. She stared into the room where both men sat slumped with their heads upon the table. Niles's face was cushioned by his food plate. She observed them for several minutes before concluding it was safe to enter. Walking quickly over to the chained prisoner, she set the bag she carried with her on the floor next to him and started to kneel down. She gasped as the man ensnared her ankle between his very large hands.

"It's okay," she murmured, gently placing her hand upon his shoulder. "I am here to help."

He blinked several times and shook his head as if trying to clear his vision or comprehend what she was saying. He eased his painful grip but kept his fingers locked around her leg.

"Thank God you are conscious," she whispered. "I have a plan, if you are willing. In exchange for your freedom, will you take me with you to the McGregor stronghold?"

The man's eyes widened, and he quickly nodded. *Too quickly, she wondered?*

She stared at him untrusting and then asked, "I have your word of honor that you will take me to the laird of the McGregors?"

"Aye, to the laird," he whispered.

"We are going to have to hurry," Alexandra said, and she took the key Aggie had given her from her pocket and proceeded to unshackle the man. "But first, let me check your injuries, as you are going to have to be able to ride."

The McGregor captive grabbed her hands as she began to run them over his body. "Later woman," he stated gruffly, "just help me to my feet."

Alexandra assisted him in rising and was staggered by his weight. She hadn't realized what a large man he was when he'd been lying down. Putting his arm about her shoulder, she picked up her bag of medicines and slowly walked him out of the hall and toward the back area of the keep where Aggie was waiting. The man's breath hissed with repressed pain from every step they took, but by the time they reached Aggie, he had grown more accustomed to it and was walking fairly well.

Aggie rushed up to them. "Hurry, I've got the back guards in the kitchen for some hot ale. I do that occasionally, but they won't stay away from their posts for long." She handed Alexandra her sling, and then she threw fur cloaks over both of them and herded them through the outer door.

"It's snowing!" Alexandra exclaimed as they stepped out into the night. *Lord, what next?*

"Hopefully it will continue and serve to cover our tracks," the McGregor said. "They'll know the direction we'll choose, but not the path."

"There are to be horses staked for us at the creek," Alexandra said as she led the way toward the closest intersection where the creek should be. The fresh layer of snow on the ground helped to reflect the light of the night and made it easier for Alexandra to get her bearings, but it would also make them more visible to the guards when they came back out. The McGregor must have also reached this same conclusion as he significantly increased his pace. No longer leaning upon her, he kept his hand at her elbow allowing her to lead. Within several minutes they were safely behind the cover of forest trees.

"It's not much farther. How are you holding up?" she asked with concern.

"I'll make it," he said through clenched teeth. The cold must be helping to keep him conscious. Finally, they broke through the trees and came upon the bubbling creek. There were no horses in sight.

"Damn," the McGregor started cursing.

"Shh!" Alexandra hissed, "Let me think." They wouldn't make much progress on foot in his condition. Envisioning the keep and the stables in her mind, she tried to imagine the path that Lem would have taken with the horses.

They both heard the faint sound of a horse's neigh at the same time. "Thank you, God!" Alexandra gave a sigh of relief. Hurrying east in the direction of the bend in the creek, they came upon the hobbled horses.

Alexandra recognized the gray mare as a horse she had ridden as a child, and the black gelding alongside looked to be as old. They were not prime horseflesh, but they would do. She knelt down to unhobble them while the McGregor held their reins. Handing Alexandra the reins to the gray mare, Ian cursed again as he carefully pulled himself up onto the back of the gelding. He was bent low over the horse but managed to maintain his seat.

Alexandra tied her bags to the saddle and mounted her own horse. Reaching her arm out toward the McGregor, she said, "Why don't you give me your horse's reins while you rest as best as you can. I will follow this creek to the end of my property, and after that you'll have to lead the way." The McGregor handed over his reins without a word.

****

The snow continued to fall as they made their way along the creek bed. The snowflakes grew bigger and floated unnaturally long in the air before they hit the ground. The forest was still, and she heard only the soft crunching of their horses' hoofs on the fresh snow and the continuous gurgle of water flowing over rocks in the burn.

Alexandra found herself once again alone with her thoughts over the gentle sway of a horse. She knew she had made the right choice by running. Though she was scared and apprehensive of what lay ahead, it couldn't possibly be any worse than what she had left behind.

The wolf pup wriggled slightly against her stomach before settling down again. He was faring much better than she could have asked for. It had been a bad day for the poor mite as well. Looking over her shoulder to check on the McGregor, she found him slumped over his saddle. She didn't know whether he was still conscious or not, but he managed to remain seated. With the hood of his cloak up and over his face, he looked like a large, snow-covered rock.

They plodded along for hours, and Alexandra was weary to the bone. She could sleep for days. Surprisingly, she didn't feel nearly as cold as she had during the ride in the rain earlier that same day, or was that yesterday? Time seemed to run all together. If she and the McGregor had both been in good health and riding good steeds, they would probably have covered twice the distance. *Thank you, God, for the snow!* It was going to be their saving grace.

As darkness faded and dawn broke, they rode beside the creek and out into a small clearing that contained several outcroppings of rocks. Alexandra stopped the horses and dismounted, shaking snow from her cloak. She walked over to the McGregor who had awakened or stirred when the horses halted. Looking up, far up, into his swollen face, she said, "This is as far as I know the way. We are at the Sullivan border. I believe the McGregor lands lie to the west of his?"

"Yes, and we are at least half a day's journey from reaching the McGregor border and then two more days before we reach the McGregor keep." He stood in the stirrups and swung his leg over the back of the gelding. "The horses are in need of a rest before we continue, and we're going to need a supply of water with us," he added as he eased himself from the saddle.

"Aggie thought of everything." Alexandra withdrew two leather canteen flasks and a bag of oats for the horses. "I should attend to your wounds now while the horses are resting."

The McGregor walked over to one of the rock outcroppings and brushed off the snow before sitting down. The snow was still falling, but it was much finer. Alexandra hobbled the horses after letting them drink from the burn and cleared a place on the ground for their oats. The McGregor watched her movements until she pulled the wolf pup out from under her cloak and set him on the ground.

"What the…?" he exclaimed as he watched the furry pup dance around her feet. She picked up the cub and gave him a quick kiss on his snout before putting him back on the ground and telling him to take care of his business. The fat pup waddled up to the edge of the creek and after testing the depth of the water with his paw began to drink. He tagged along behind as she walked over to where the McGregor sat. The McGregor stared at the pup as it sniffed around his boots, and then he looked back at the woman who was busy pulling items from her bag.

"It's a wolf. Are you daft?" he asked.

Looking straight into his one semi-open brown eye, she replied with a smile, "Yes."

Lifting a ball of material from her bag, she said, "I'm pretty sure you have some broken or cracked ribs. They'll feel much better if you let me wrap them, but you'll have to remove your shirt in this cold." She looked at him and lifted her brows.

The McGregor stood up and shrugged off the fur cloak and started to pull off his woolen shirt. His breath caught when he lifted his hands up over his head. Alexandra moved closer and helped him pull the garment off. His chest and arms were massively muscled and covered with black and blue welts. She could not help but stare before she came to her senses and started unrolling the material.

"Please sit back down, I'll be able to reach you better," Alexandra said. As he did so, she stepped up and stood between his open knees. She could barely reach around him to wrap the cloth. Each time she stretched a portion of cloth around his back, she had to stand uncomfortably close to his chest with her arms wrapped around him. She could feel his warm breath on the top of her head. Embarrassed, she hurriedly finished her task. Stepping back and finding her own breath, she said, "I'm sorry, I know that had to hurt."

"On the contrary, I was pleasantly distracted." He picked up and shook his discarded filthy shirt and slowly brought it down over his head. This time Alexandra let him struggle with it on his own. Her cheeks flushed, she turned her back on him and put several things back into her bag. She had herbs that could help with his pain, but they would also make him sleepy. Better to wait until they were camped for the evening. The wolf pup grabbed at the hem of her skirt and growled and tugged it back and forth.

"I'll bet you're hungry, my friend," she said and threw him a piece of dried meat, which immediately grabbed his attention. She turned and gave the McGregor a large piece of dried meat and a hunk of bread before starting to eat her own portion. While they ate, the McGregor kept staring at her like he was trying to fathom a puzzle.

"Must you stare at me while I'm eating?" Alexandra pulled the bread away from her mouth and waited.

"But the view is so pleasing." The McGregor shifted his weight on the rock and continued to stare, smiling now.

Feeling unsettled by his teasing, Alexandra pocketed what remained of her food to eat later and walked toward the forest with the intent of relieving herself.

"Don't go beyond calling distance," the McGregor shouted from behind her.

Chapter Three

As they pressed on, the McGregor led the way, and he took her reins as well. The pup had settled down almost immediately as if the rocking motion of the horse helped put him to sleep. The snow continued to fall, and the temperature seemed to be dropping with it, either that or the coldness was starting to really get to her. She was glad the McGregor had taken control of her horse as she could drop off to sleep at any moment. Only the thought of falling from the horse kept her awake.

Alexandra wondered if Niles had wakened and if they were being pursued yet. Would he just send his men, or would he ride with them? He was going to have a major headache when he woke for which she was exceedingly glad. Niles would be infuriated at being crossed. Would he immediately notice she was also missing, or would he think the McGregor escaped on his own? Knowing Niles, he would think she had something to do with his problems.

Her thoughts turned toward the freed McGregor. She would have to ask his name. She couldn't just keep thinking of him as 'the McGregor.' What was his position in the clan? His teasing and the way he watched her were disturbing. She didn't have much experience with men as she had been living at the abbey since she was young, but her instincts told her she needn't fear this McGregor as she had Niles. He disturbed her on a totally different level.

The feel of the dagger she kept in her boot gave her some comfort. She had started wearing one soon after Niles's failed rape attempt even though she was living at the abbey. It brought her comfort and peace of mind. In fact, she often practiced throwing the blade at trees when she took long walks looking for herbs to replenish her dwindling supplies. It was surprising how many times the knife came in handy for different purposes, and by now she considered it a useful tool.

They trudged on in silence in the deepening snow throughout the early morning hours and into the afternoon. The horses had to work harder, high-stepping through the growing drifts. To her surprise, she nodded off several times but jolted awake as soon as she started to slip from the center of her horse's back.

Several short stops gave the horses breaks. Alexandra took those opportunities to let the pup down after clearing a place in the snow with her boots so that he could move about freely and relieve himself.

The McGregor seemed to be holding up very well, though she hoped they weren't lost, as he paused periodically to view the landscape. She didn't know how he could tell where he was going. The sun was not out to tell them east from west, and the forest looked all the same to her.

Finally the snow tapered off, but soon after it stopped, the wind began to pick up. Icy particles swirled in the air around them, and she pulled the fur cloak tight about her face. She could barely keep her eyes open against the pelting sting.

"We've been on McGregor land for the last hour," the McGregor shouted back over the whistling wind. "There is a hunting shelter close to here, if we don't miss it. Be on the lookout."

Either the McGregor was really good at his directions or extremely lucky, for they rode almost directly into the path that led to a wood framed structure. A three-sided lean-to, that she assumed was meant for animals, was positioned next to it, and the McGregor led the way in. They worked together to take care of the horses and feed them before entering what reminded her of a crofter's hut.

Alexandra was surprised to see that the shelter was in fairly decent shape. There were no windows, only the door they entered through. A crude fireplace stood against the opposite wall. Little light was available once the door was shut; only that which seeped in through the cracks in the ceiling and walls, but it was enough to see by once her eyes adjusted. Along one of the side walls was a supply of cut wood. A couple of make-shift chairs made from saplings sat in the center of the room. A battered cooking pot and several utensils lay on the hearth in front of the fireplace.

The McGregor set her bags down on one of the chairs. "Do you have any flint in these for starting a fire?" he asked.

"I don't know. I haven't been through all the stuff Aggie packed," she said as she knelt by the hearth and began to empty the bags. She pulled out dried meat, bread, a hunk of cheese, a bag of oats, pouch of sugar, a couple tin cups and bowls, and then, from the bottom of the bag, she pulled out a flint stone and several candles.

"I swear, if your Aggie were here, I'd give her a

big, fat kiss," he said and took the flint from her hands and went to load wood in the fireplace. While the McGregor worked on building a fire, Alexandra took the struggling pup from his pouch and sat him on the ground. He began to sniff the dirt floor and explore the room, so she packed the food back into the bags before he had a chance to discover it.

The wind howled and whistled outside the hut. Now and again a small flurry of snow blew into the room from the cracks. She thanked God for the shelter that provided them safety from the storm. Alexandra doubted they would have survived without it. She couldn't imagine being out in this weather alone, and she might have been, if she hadn't been able to rouse the McGregor. She thanked God again, this time for providing a knowledgeable traveling companion.

Alexandra paced the room, rubbing her hands together and blowing on them. She shivered. She hoped a fire would significantly warm the hut. She picked up the pup and held him close, wondering if he too was cold. But he would have none of it and struggled until she let him free. Obviously the cold did not bother him.

Tired, she quit pacing and dropped down in one of the chairs to watch the McGregor while he worked. He really was an impressively big man. His dark brown hair was thick and overly long, reaching his broad shoulders. His massive hands were not the least bit awkward or bumbling as he carefully tented wood shavings and twigs. The pup came up several times to investigate, and each time he did, the man gave him a twig of his own before brushing him aside once more. With utmost patience, he stroked the flint again and again, until finally a spark ignited one of the shavings, and it began to curl and smoke. Cupping his hands, the McGregor gently blew on the wood shaving until it caught fire and then added other shavings one by one until he had a little fire started.

Alexandra melted snow in the cook pot and made some mint tea from her bag of herbs. They dipped their tin cups into the pot to refill them as needed. The fire now blazed brightly, and they positioned their chairs as close to it as they could. The heat was heavenly. Alexandra pushed her feet forward as close to the fire as she dared and kept her hands wrapped around the hot cup. When holding the cup against her lips, the steam from it warmed her face. She glanced at the McGregor and discovered he was watching her again.

"I don't even know your name. What is it?" she asked.

"Ian McGregor of the McGregor clan." He lifted his head high.

"What is your position in the clan? Aggie said you were alone when you were caught. Are you a guard?"

"Aye, I guess you could say that, but I'm also one of the clan's best hunters."

"Is your laird an honorable man?" She asked the question that weighed most heavily on her mind.

Ian added another log to the fire. "Do you mean is he a better man than those two lazy peacocks we've escaped from? Aye. He is a fair man, but many fear him. He will relish the thought of going to battle against the Sullivan clan and your cousin." He looked at her to gauge her reaction.

"My cousin, as you know, is an evil man, but the innocent people on the estate, such as Aggie, I care very much about."

"You'll get your chance to plead your case to the laird. Who knows, he just might take a liking to you," Ian said with a grin.

Alexandra hoped he didn't take too much of a liking to her. She had enough problems.

"Tell me more about this Niles. How did you come to be in his care?"

"My parents died in a carriage accident when I was twelve. Niles is my second cousin and last blood relative. He became my guardian and the estate manager. He's an evil snake. Not to be trusted in any way." She emphasized her statement by meeting his eyes before looking back in the fire.

"I'd only met him once before, when I was five. His parents sent him to visit for the summer. He was thirteen. I was so thrilled when I heard the news. It would be like having a big brother, the sibling I'd always wanted." She paused and the McGregor's silence encouraged her to continue.

"It didn't take long for that naïve bubble to burst. First it was small things like chasing me with spiders. I told on him of course, but my parents assured me he was just doing 'boy things.' He cornered me the next day. He held a squirming rat by its tail and swung it back and forth in my face. Then he laughed and slammed it repeatedly against the wall until it was bloody and lifeless. Throwing the carcass at me, he said that's what happens to rats."

"It was a horrible summer. His torments increased from putting deadly surprises in my bed to pushing me down a flight of stairs and breaking my arm. I cried in relief when he left." She stared into the fire as if mesmerized.

"I can still see my mother trying to comfort me by telling me not to be too sad. Niles could come visit another year." She stopped talking lost in her thoughts. Forcing the door to her memories shut, she said, "He had me so petrified I never did tell them."

She didn't want to think about Niles anymore. Changing the subject, she asked, "Would you like me to give you something for your pain? It may make you sleepy."

The McGregor was silent for a moment as if wanting her to continue, but he allowed the topic to drop and answered her question, "I'm fine, woman. I've suffered much worse in battle."

"Well, you don't look fine; in fact, you look like you've been trampled half to death. Your face is a mess, and your nose appears broken," she stated.

"It's not the first time it's been broken"—his hand automatically touched his nose—"and it probably won't be the last."

"Seeing how pig-headed you are, I imagine you're right," she quipped before giving up arguing with him.

Ian chuckled aloud. "How about some food, woman! Or are you planning on letting me starve to death?"

Alexandra took the food from the bags and dispersed cheese, bread, and more strips of dried meat. She also gave the pup a strip of meat. They ate in silence as they savored the meager fare. The sun had gone down, and no more light filtered in through the cracks. Ian added wood to the fire, and it burned brightly. Occasionally, sparks popped and flew toward them. Shadows danced around the room.

Listening to the whistling wind that had yet to die

down, Ian said, "The temperature is still dropping. We are going to have to share some body heat tonight, as well as keep this fire burning."

Alexandra stared at him for several seconds before saying, "Surely that's not necessary."

"Aye, it is. We have a long night ahead of us, and we both need solid rest before we continue on the next leg of our journey. We'll not spend the night awake and shivering."

Eyes wide, Alexandra continued to stare at him.

"Woman. I'll not be taking no for an answer. We'll both be fully clothed, and as you've already pointed out, I'm in no condition to attack you." As he spoke, he stood and added several more logs to the fire, stoking it up. Taking off his cloak, he spread it out on the dirt floor near the fireplace. He picked up one of her bags and tossed it onto the cloak before lying down and using the bag as a pillow. He held out his hand to her, inviting her onto the makeshift bed.

Alexandra looked at him hesitantly for several seconds before removing her own fur cloak. Ignoring his hand, she slowly sat down beside him and tossed her cloak over them both before lying down on her side, being careful not to touch him.

Ian put an arm around her waist and ignoring her gasp, pulled her stiff body up against his, in spoon fashion. Putting his right arm under her head for a pillow and keeping his left hand securely around her waist, he whispered in her ear, "Isn't that better?" Alexandra didn't reply. It *was* better, even though her stomach was fluttering. His warmth was already enveloping her. Surprisingly, the hard length of his body surrounding her made her feel safe. The strain of the last few days caught up, and she drifted off to sleep while reciting her evening prayers.

****

Ian lay awake. The feel of Alexandra's small bottom tight against his loins made his blood boil. Visions of her naked and stretched out in front of the fire made him want to remove her clothes and climb astride her. Taking deep breaths, he reminded himself he was a man of honor. He knew she had been sent from the abbey as he had listened to Sullivan and her cousin's conversation throughout the day while he'd been chained to the floor like a dog. Alexandra's whole demeanor shouted of innocence; she was as different from her cousin as night is from day.

The rare combination of her beauty and innocence captivated him. Never had he felt such a strong, immediate attraction, but he did not plan on falling under any woman's spell. Memories of his father's decline after his mother's death served to remind him what pain and grief could do to a man. His father, the strong tower of his sons' lives, had crumbled like flamed kindling, and he had sunk into a spiral of teary depression and drunkenness until his death. His father's lack of leadership had almost destroyed his clan. Witnessing his brother's disastrous marriage reinforced Ian's decision not to lose his heart to a woman. Enjoy their company, aye, and accept what was freely offered, but no more.

He steered his thoughts to Niles Conrad and the Sullivan. Thoughts of blood-thirsty battle and revenge calmed his spirit. Curled protectively around Alexandra's soft warm body, he too drifted off to sleep.

****

The pup, awakened by hunger, started licking Alexandra's face. She woke with a jolt to a sitting position and elbowed Ian in his side in the process. Cursing, Ian held a hand to his ribs before he sat up also.

"I'm so sorry!" Alexandra exclaimed, reaching out to him.

"Glad you waited until morning to do that." Ian stiffly shoved his hand out, palm open, as if to keep her away. He jumped to his feet and walked to the dying fire.

Alexandra pulled the wolf cub onto her lap and held him close. She was amazed she had slept so well. Since the summons had come from Niles, she'd been unable to sleep peacefully.

Ian tended the embers and said, "We need to get moving this morning. The wind has died down, and Sullivan and Conrad will be searching for us. They will probably divide their men into groups of two and three to cast a wider net. One beaten man with a woman will not seem too big of a challenge for a small group, even if we had weapons." He paused and she looked up at him from the floor to find him watching her try to tame her hair into a braid.

"I'm sorry. I should have considered that we would need weapons."

"Most women wouldn't," he answered, continuing to stare.

"I am not most women." She blushed under his disconcerting gaze. "My father always wanted a son. He took me hunting. He taught me how to use a bow and arrow, and even had a set made just for me when I was ten. I should have thought of it."

"You already had much to consider." He pulled a cloak from the floor. "I'll get the horses ready."

Frigid air entered the room as he went out with the pup trailing at his feet. Alexandra hurried to make breakfast from their oats before packing everything back up. When Ian returned a few minutes later, he appeared surprised to find a steaming bowl of porridge waiting. They ate their meal beside the dying embers of the fire. The food was pretty tasteless, Alexandra thought, but it did serve to fill their stomachs. The pup licked their bowls clean before she put them away, and she made a mental note to herself to remember to wash them well.

The day was just dawning when they mounted the horses. A hushed stillness lay around them as if the snow absorbed all sound. Alexandra held her own reins and followed after Ian. In some places, the wind had completely blown the snow from the ground leaving it bare, while in other spots, the horses had to barrel through the high snowdrifts. Her horse had the easier go of it since the mare could follow in the gelding's path.

When the sun came up, the forest transformed into an enchanted place. Snow glittered like jewels hanging from the trees, and in the bright sunlight, the top layer of snow on the ground sparkled like diamonds. And although it was cold, the sun felt much better against her face than the wind had.

As they rode, Alexandra's thoughts went back to her childhood and the happy times she'd had with her parents playing in the snow. They'd loved her and indulged her. Her father had treated her like a son much to her mother's dismay. He'd taught her how to ride and shoot with the bow and arrow until she was proficient. Her mother, on the other hand, made sure she knew how to dress and how to act like a lady. She had received the best of both worlds.

They pushed on as fast as they dared, much the same as the day before, only without the falling snow. When the horses appeared to be tiring, Ian stopped for a short break. During those times, they all stretched their legs or took a few bites of food before mounting up again.

Alexandra's bottom hadn't become accustomed to all the riding yet, and it grew increasingly sore as the day progressed. When they stopped again around midday, she was thankful to be getting off her horse. She took the pup from his pouch and set him on a bare patch of ground. Happy to be unconfined, he took off running in circles before attempting to jump over and through some of the smaller snow drifts.

Ian pointed up to a tree-sparse ridge to the north and said, "I'm going to walk up there to get my bearings. The horses could use a longer break. Don't stray far from this spot." Without waiting for a response, he strode through the drifted snow toward the ridge.

Alexandra gave the horses a handful of grain each before giving herself and the pup a slice of dried meat. She then headed into the trees in the opposite direction to the one Ian had taken. She felt more at ease relieving herself knowing he was not close by. The pup as usual tagged along behind and kept her in his sights while he played and investigated his surroundings.

Straightening her skirts, Alexandra was stepping out from behind a bush when she heard the pup growl. She couldn't see him, but he sounded close. Hoping he was just playing and hadn't put himself in any danger, she hurried in the direction of the noise. She ran about twenty feet farther into the thick forest before she stopped abruptly. The pup was hunched and growling at three rough-looking men on horseback who were attempting to surround him. As soon as she had burst into view, their attention shifted to her.

Assessing the situation in an instant, she turned and fled in the direction from which she had come. She could hear their shouts and the horses tearing through the brush behind her. Her heart pounding, she ran as fast as she could, holding her skirts high off the ground and jumping over the drifts. The snow muffled the sound of hoof beats, but she could hear them getting closer, and then a hand closed on the back of her scalp, jerking her painfully to a stop.

Frightened, she screamed at the top of her lungs while turning and twisting to pummel the side of the horse and the rider's leg with her fists. The animal, startled by her screaming and her attack, reared, and Alexandra felt the sudden release of her hair as the rider was unseated. Once more she took off running, but she didn't get far before something heavy knocked her forward off her feet, and she flew face first into the snow. The impact momentarily took the breath from her body. She pushed herself over onto her back just in time to see the fist that slammed into her face before she blacked out.

Chapter Four

Alexandra woke up to find herself lying on her belly over the back of her own swaying horse. Her hands and feet were bound and tied to the stirrups. Her head pounded with each movement of the animal. She tried to speak but found she couldn't as a rag was stuffed in her mouth. Nausea rose in her throat, and she stifled a gag.

Turning her head to both sides, she saw her mare's reins held by the rider in front of her, and Ian's horse led by the captor in the front position. Behind her, she glimpsed the pup running in the distance trying to keep up. They were traveling in single file with her horse bringing up the rear.

She heard her captors arguing over the best way to capture the McGregor clansman. The man in the lead wanted to follow the tracks Ian had left in the snow, while one of the others argued they should have set a trap and waited for Ian to come back.

Alexandra hoped she hadn't been unconscious for long. She had no way of knowing how far they were from where she and Ian had stopped to rest. Questions ran through her mind. What would Ian do when he discovered her and the horses missing? Was he close by? Had he seen the riders from the ridge? Would he continue toward the McGregor stronghold alone and on foot?

Her thoughts were startled when a blood-curdling war cry pierced the air. The McGregor charged from behind one of the nearby trees and jumped up. With both hands, he grabbed the back of the captor who was leading her horse and flung him off his saddle. From that point on, everything happened so quickly that time passed in a blur. The McGregor pulled the falling man's dagger from his belt and killed him with it by the time he hit the ground. Then the McGregor snatched the downed man's hatchet and threw it at the next captor in line, who had just turned his horse around to see what was happening. The hatchet struck the second man dead center in his chest. The McGregor grabbed the handle of the embedded hatchet and used it to drag him from his horse and onto the ground. Standing with one foot braced against the man's chest, he used both hands to pry the bloody hatchet loose, before he darted after the lead man who had turned his horse around again in order to flee in the opposite direction. The McGregor grasped the reins of the second rider's horse, swung himself up into the saddle and chased after the fleeing man. Within seconds, both men were out of view.

Alexandra, her heart thundering in her chest and ears, could not believe what had just happened. The McGregor, like a wild beast, had disarmed and killed two of her captors before they barely had time to realize what was happening. Still dangling upside down from her horse, she had viewed everything from a dizzying, distorted point of view. Her horse had whinnied and side-stepped out of the way, but the mare had not wandered off. Alexandra listened for sounds from the forest and prayed it would be the McGregor who came back for her.

Waiting tensely, she watched the wolf pup investigate the bodies of the two men who darkened the snow. He growled low in his throat and hesitantly sniffed around them, before he padded toward her. The pup jumped up to reach her, but only succeeded in startling the horse into shying away. The mare was used to the smell of the wolf pup since he had been riding with her, but what if the pup's antics got him kicked or made the horse bolt? Neither option was good. As the pup crouched again ready to spring, Alexandra used a stern tone and yelled "No!" through the gag. He stopped mid-crouch and turned his head sideways as if trying to understand. Before he could jump again, they both heard the hoof beats of a rider coming back.

Holding her breath until she could see who it was, Alexandra let out a muffled sigh of relief when the McGregor trotted up, towing the third man's horse behind. The wolf pup ran forward to greet him when he dismounted. The McGregor's cloak and hands were stained with blood, and he stopped and washed them in the snow before he picked up the pup and strode toward Alexandra's horse. Talking to the pup, he said, "What do you think, shall we leave her this way until we reach the keep?"

Glaring at him, Alexandra wiggled and tried to talk through the gag. The McGregor simply threw back his head and laughed, and then smacked her bottom with his free hand. As Alexandra squirmed and made indignant noises, he took his newly acquired dagger in hand and cut the ropes that kept her hands tied to the stirrup before he walked back around the horse to cut the rope that tethered her feet.

He wrapped his free arm around her waist and

assisted her in sliding backward off the horse, and then he cut the cord that tied her feet together. Turning her around, he pulled the dirty rag from her mouth. Alexandra tried to make a cutting remark but found her throat so dry all she could do was emit a croak, which only served to make the McGregor roar with laughter again.

As she turned to walk away, Ian stepped in her path and gently tilted her head up. She winced as his fingertips brushed the hair from her cheek. A black scowl appeared on his face. Alexandra opened her mouth to say something, but the dark look in his eyes made her hold her tongue.

The McGregor walked among the slain men and took the remaining weapons from their bodies. He offered Alexandra a dagger which she declined as she already had the one that he didn't know about. He looked surprised when she pointed to a bow and quiver. "May I have that if you don't need it?"

"Only if you promise not to point it anywhere in my direction," he answered with a grin and handed the bow to her.

"We'll start out riding their horses since they are younger and won't get as tired, and then we'll switch to keep up a good pace. I imagine the others will know the direction we've taken once these three don't show up at a designated meeting time." He brought over one of her captors' horses and handed her the reins. He locked his hands together to give her a foot up, but she just stood there dazed and frowned at him.

"Aren't we going to give them a proper Christian burial?" she asked.

"No," he stated flatly. Before she could protest, he

unlocked his hands and put them around her waist and lifted her up onto the horse.

Seeing him wince as he did this, Alexandra asked, "How could you fight the way you just did when you are so recently injured?"

"In battle lust, the pain ceases to exist. I've known men who were mortally wounded but didn't even realize they'd been hurt until after the fighting was over. Besides, I come from good stock and heal quickly."

Alexandra shook her head in amazement, and they started riding at a brisk pace. She estimated there was probably half a day's ride left before the sun set. The gelding she rode was frisky but manageable. Once again, she followed as the McGregor led the way.

They covered ground quickly, even with frequent breaks to change horses. The pup settled down and remained quiet. He must have exhausted himself trying to keep up with her horse when she was captive.

During the ride, Alexandra thought about how close she had come to being back in Niles's hands. She thanked God for her escape and for giving her a protector, even if that protector just wanted to get back the horses and supplies. She prayed for the souls of the three dead men, but she prayed most of all for the McGregor's soul for having killed them. She was confused over the matter. She knew there were battles all through the Bible, with God's people on one side and their enemy on the other, but she also knew that one of the ten commandments was 'Thou shall not kill.'

Watching Ian's back as they rode, she noted how tall he was in the saddle and how easily he negotiated his way through the snow. He was an enigma to her.

She found she thought of him as Ian when he teased her or gently handled the pup, and as the McGregor when he exhibited the proud, warrior side of his personality.

When they next changed horses, Alexandra asked wearily, "Will we reach the McGregor keep this evening?"

"Nay," he replied and mounted the old gelding, "we'll hold up tonight at another hunting hut. If all goes well, we'll reach the McGregor keep before noon tomorrow."

Alexandra nodded her understanding and mounted her old mare. Although she was nervous about her reception when they reached the keep, she was ready to be done with all this. What she wouldn't give to soak in a steamy bath and to have squeaky, clean hair.

****

Night approached, and they still had not reached the hut. As the warmth of the sun disappeared, the temperature dropped dramatically. The McGregor took her reins again because it was difficult to follow him in the dark. There was no moonlight to brighten the snow, but somehow he knew exactly where he was going, and it wasn't long before they came upon another shelter. This one had an enclosed shed for the horses. Thankfully, extra grain had been in the bags of the slain men, and as before, they cared for the horses before entering the hut.

The interior was very dark, but Ian was familiar enough with its layout that he moved about and started a fire. Alexandra stood just inside the doorway and waited until it was light enough for her to see before she stepped in to investigate. The hut was similar to the last one, except it also had a table and a pile of straw in one corner.

Alexandra put the supplies she carried on the table and emptied the unfamiliar bags they'd taken from the three horsemen. She found they contained food, much the same as the fare they already had, with the exception of several dried apples and some beans. Her stomach growled loudly, and she put her hand against it and glanced at the McGregor. He grinned. "I'm hungry too, lass. At least we don't have to worry about running out of food." He pulled up a chair to the wobbly table.

They ate in relative silence, eating this time until their stomachs were satisfied. The pup was also given a larger portion of meat. The dried apples were slightly tart, but tasted delicious. When they finished, Alexandra repacked the remaining food, and Ian took the fireplace cookpot outside to fill with snow.

Once again they found themselves huddled before a fire sipping on hot herbal tea. The wolf pup entertained them by acting wild and crazy. He ran around the room chasing shadows and growling. He ran back and skidded to a stop at their feet. Alexandra was utterly surprised when Ian got down on the floor and played with him. Teasing the animal with a one-inch diameter stick, he let the pup grab one end and then shook the stick and tried to take it back. The pup clamped onto it and refused to release his prize. Alexandra laughed when Ian picked up the stick and swung the puppy in the air. Dropping the pup onto his lap, he pried the piece of wood from his mouth and threw it across the room. The pup sprinted after it and brought it back, nudging the wood into Ian's hands.

"What are you going to name this rascal?" he asked and threw the stick one more time.

"I don't know, he's certainly very happy, isn't he? Maybe that's what I should call him, Happy."

"Happy?" He laughed. "Are you kidding? For a wolf? What about Warrior or Killer or Beast? You know, you're never going to be able to tame him."

Alexandra smiled. "I'm not going to try to tame him. I'd let him loose right now if I thought he'd live. I guess I'll take it one day at a time. What's wrong with the name Happy? I think it'll suit him just fine."

"Aye, I can see your point. Meet Happy, he'll happily tear your leg off, or I see Happy's happy to be covered in the blood of his enemy," Ian joked.

Alexandra clapped her hands and whistled. "Here Happy!"

The wolf pup dropped his stick and trotted over to her. He turned his head inquisitively, and she laughed, reaching down to pet him. "See, he likes his new name."

****

Ian moved the straw from the corner of the room and spread it in front of the fireplace. He kicked through the pile several times to separate and fluff it up. She moved the chairs back to their original position by the table while Ian stoked the fire one last time before they went to sleep. After he arranged his fur cloak over the bed of straw, Ian lay down and extended his hand just as he had the previous night. This time she didn't hesitate. She placed her hand in his to steady herself as she sat down and spread her cloak.

Ian wrapped his arm around her waist and pulled her to him. He tucked her close in front of his body with her head pillowed on his arm. Alexandra was surprised how much softer the floor was with the straw under them. She was also very aware of Ian's hard body pressed against her. His breath brushed her neck, and tingles ran up and down her spine. She was not nearly as tired tonight, and it was hard to relax and to keep still. Was Ian sleeping? He was a strange man. She was amazed someone so large, who fought so ruthlessly, could also be very gentle. Did he have any family?

"Stop fidgeting, woman."

"I'm sorry." She shifted to yet another position. "I'm not very tired tonight."

"Why don't you tell me more of this Niles?"

She was silent, considering whether to open herself up to the pain of remembering. Perhaps the more he knew, the more he could help her convince his laird of the nature of the man who plotted against them both. Where to begin?

"I was devastated when my parents died. Niles arrived shortly after their burial. Pleased by his good fortune, he strutted around like a gloating peacock. He took control immediately. He fired staff that had lived their whole lives on the estate. Several were beaten or flogged for imaginary crimes and replaced by people he knew. The more I protested, the more he seemed to enjoy it. He locked me in my room for weeks at a time with little to eat for punishment. The butler was caught sneaking me bread. Niles accused him of thievery and had his right hand cut off." Her throat tightened at the memory.

"I felt so guilty and blamed myself. I don't know what happened to the poor man after he was thrown off the estate." She paused, wondering if there was a way she could find him and apologize.

Ian's arm squeezed her waist and he said, "I'm

sorry."

"After that, the servants left as soon as they could. Only a few brave ones like Aggie stayed on. I began catching him looking at me with both hatred and lust. I told you I was twelve?" she asked.

"To make a long story short, one of the young maids was found dead on the property. Her naked body was discovered beaten and broken. Niles made a big speech about how the killer would be hunted down and brought to justice, but he looked at me and smiled, and I knew. I knew he was responsible."

"I started placing large objects in front of my bedroom door. It was the only way I could sleep. One night, despite the obstacles, he broke into my room. He was drunk, luckily for me, but I still couldn't get away. When it came down to it, he couldn't..." Alexandra struggled to find the right words and waved her hand in the air, "perform..."

"I understand," Ian said dryly.

"He was furious and pummeled me with his fists. My last thought before I passed out was that I was going to die. The only reason he didn't kill me is that if I die before I marry, the entire estate goes to the church. He would have lost everything."

"So he is a coward who preys on the young and innocent," the McGregor said through gritted teeth.

"Yes," she whispered.

"You are safe now. Put your mind at ease and rest," he said.

Eventually, her mind quieted. She was warm and secure in his arms. She woke in the morning to find she was not facing away from Ian but was nestled with her face against his neck. Somehow, her right leg had come to lie between his thighs. Mortified, she slowly tried to withdraw it without waking him. He stirred a little and turned toward her, effectually trapping her leg and most of her lower body under him. Murmuring something unintelligible, he started nibbling along her neck and up her jaw. *Sweet Lord, that feels so good.* Moving from her jaw, his lips closed over her mouth, and he caressed her with his tongue before slipping it into her mouth to stroke hers. Ian pulled her tighter under him with one arm, while the other hand moved up to cover her breast. A jolt of sensation went straight to her lower stomach and served to break her paralysis.

"Stop!" she said breathlessly and pushed against his chest with both hands.

He was an unmovable rock. With a deep sigh, he hung his head and rested his forehead against her shoulder briefly before he rolled over onto his back. He flung one arm across his face and didn't move other than to continue breathing deeply.

Alexandra scooted backward out from under the cloak as fast as she could until she could stand. She too was breathless. She watched him warily, but he remained motionless, his face hidden from her view. Abruptly, he stood up and without looking at her, stalked out of the hut. Alexandra froze and stared at the closed door. He hadn't taken a cloak out with him, so he probably wouldn't be gone long.

Gathering her wits, she started packing their belongings. The wolf pup ran circles around her while she made porridge from the oats and leftover apples. Minutes later, the McGregor returned and announced the horses were ready. She glanced at him when she pushed a bowl of food his way and noted he was already acting as if nothing had happened. They ate in uncomfortable silence. Alexandra felt the need to talk about it, but she didn't know exactly how to broach the subject.

The sun was rising over the horizon as they led the horses from the shed. They began the day riding the older horses. Alexandra followed holding the reins of one, while the McGregor held the other two. This day was warmer by far than the last two days. Spring was still a month or two away, but she was already heartily sick of the snow and cold. Wishing for the smell of green grass and fragrant flowers, she imagined what her surroundings would look like on a fair summer's day.

She watched the McGregor's tall back as they rode and tried to keep her thoughts away from that morning, but the memory flooded back. She was having a hard time accepting how he had made her feel so alive and on fire. The only other person to have touched her so intimately was Niles, and that whole incident left her scarred and uninterested in knowing more about what happened between men and women, which was probably why it was such a surprise to know that Ian's touch made her feel so different. She never expected to have to fight her own feelings. Her life was planned out, she reminded herself. She wanted to be a nun and live in peace at the abbey with the other women, serving God by helping the sick and the poor.

The McGregor did not talk much, and only when he needed to convey information about the upcoming trail. Alexandra wondered if he was angry. It was undoubtedly a good thing they would be arriving at the McGregor keep that very day, God willing. But how often would she see him?

After several hours of riding, they broke through the trees and onto a large rolling meadow that was at least a mile long and half a mile wide. The McGregor called a halt, and they took a break at the meadow's edge. The open field looked like a lake. The wind had blown patterns of waves, like crests on water. Alexandra played her imaginary game and envisioned how beautiful the field would be in the summertime covered with tall blowing grass, dancing wildflowers, and a multitude of butterflies. She lifted Happy from his pouch and set him to run free while she stretched her legs.

The McGregor stared at the tree-lined meadow and appeared to be watching for something. She looked at him inquisitively.

"We'll change mounts now." It was an order. "I don't like making us vulnerable out in the open, but we'll also save a lot of time cutting through rather than going around."

Alexandra nodded and gathered the pup. She mounted the young gelding she'd ridden the day before. He danced with her extra weight before settling. They trotted side by side into the meadow, the horses high-stepping through the larger snow drifts. They reached midpoint in the field, when she heard the McGregor curse.

Looking over at him, she saw his attention was to his left. There, coming out of the west side of the woods, were ten riders galloping straight toward them.

Chapter Five

Alexandra froze with terror at the sight of the riders heading for them before she heard the McGregor yell, "Drop the mare's reins and ride as fast as you can toward the trees on our right."

She let go of the reins to the extra horse she was leading and kicked the gelding she rode hard in his sides. He bolted and took off at a gallop. Hanging on tight to his mane, she hunched low over his neck and urged him on. Glancing to her left, she saw the McGregor was keeping up with her, but he hung back at her flank. The tree line was fast approaching. Not daring to look, she wondered how far away the other riders were.

As soon as they crossed into the trees, the McGregor yelled for her to pull up. She reined in the horse and turned to face him. He had already dismounted and strode toward her.

"Keep riding north as fast as you dare without killing your horse. The McGregor keep is no more than hours away," he shouted, "I'll keep them at bay as long as I can. Ask for my brother, James McGregor, and tell him everything."

Alexandra looked down at the man who had helped save her. How could she just leave him?

"Do as I say!" he shouted and slapped his hand on her horse's rump. "Go!"

Startled, the horse took off into the woods. Within moments, she regained control of the animal and reined him to a stop. *Dear Lord, what should I do? The McGregor doesn't know that I might be able to help him...and besides, who did he think he was to order her about?* Making up her mind, she turned her horse around and headed back.

She didn't arrive at the exact spot but found she was farther to the north when she reached the meadow. The riders were almost upon the McGregor, who just stood there like an idiot waiting for them, with a weapon in each hand, and his back to the woods. Alexandra grabbed the bow and quiver of arrows and jumped from her horse. Bracing herself against a tree trunk, she withdrew an arrow. The riders formed a circle around the McGregor.

She pulled back on the bow string and said a quick prayer. *Please God, let my aim be true, and don't let me kill anyone.* Gently letting the bowstring roll over her fingertips, she let the arrow fly toward the back shoulder of the rider nearest to her. He stiffened suddenly and slumped over his horse's neck, before falling off its right side. As the man hit the ground, she placed the next arrow ready in the bow.

The hunting party had started their attack just as Alexandra's arrow hit the first man. She pierced her third man before the rest of the group realized the McGregor was not alone. They split what was left of their forces, leaving three men to deal with the McGregor, while the last two turned and charged her position.

****

Ian McGregor had planned to disable at least half

the group before retreating into the woods and picking the rest off one at a time. His experience had taught him that men tended to drop their guard when they had a man clearly outnumbered. When the first arrow struck, Ian knew the foolish woman had not listened to him. Charging into the crowd, he easily killed two of his enemies, using one of their horses as a shield before striking down the next. He cursed when the group split and two broke off, charging in the direction of the flying arrows.

Left with three men to deal with, Ian felt an urgency to dispatch them as quickly as possible in order to go to Alexandra's aid. He was fighting the last man when he heard a faint scream. His opponent took advantage of Ian's momentary distraction and went to deal him a fatal blow. Turning his body at the last second, Ian grimaced as the man's hatchet sliced through his left arm from shoulder to elbow. Instead of retreating, he stepped into the man and stabbed him with his dagger.

****

As the two men charged Alexandra, she nervously nocked one last arrow and let it fly. The arrow landed in the nearest man's thigh. He slowed down but kept coming. Alexandra fled into the forest. The bow wasn't meant for close fighting. *Now what?* She didn't have a plan. She needed to hide, but how? She was leaving tracks in the snow, and she didn't have much time. Then an idea hit her. She stopped and retraced her footsteps, stepping exactly where she had left footprints.

She kept Happy quiet in his pouch, but she knew it was only a matter of minutes before they reached her hiding spot. She needed to buy some time for the McGregor to find her.

She watched the first man break through the tree-line with his sword drawn. Peering at the ground from atop his horse, he followed her path in the snow. The second man, cursing loudly and pressing his hand against his bleeding thigh, soon caught up to him. The first man led the way, following her tracks until they abruptly ended.

"Where did she go? Her tracks just disappeared?"

"We'll find the witch, and she'll pay when we do," his companion muttered and wrapped a cloth around his leg.

When they circled under her tree, Happy struggled in earnest. She held his wiggling body tight against her with one hand and clamped the other around his snout. But Happy still managed to emit a loud growl. Both men stared up into the tree.

She looked down at their astonished faces and climbed even higher. Who would have thought having been such a tomboy as a child would come in so handy one day?

The two men below looked at one another before the injured man shrugged and said, "I can't climb with this leg."

The other man, shorter and stockier, stood in his saddle and grabbed a branch. Pulling himself up into the tree, he started to ascend. As he climbed, the injured man below shouted threats of what they would do when they got their hands on her. Alexandra concentrated on not slipping on the snowy bark and climbed higher. The man following her was making faster progress without the hindrance of skirts. The branches were getting smaller and smaller, and instead of continuing to climb, she carefully slid sideways, out on the current limb as far as she dared go, while using both hands to hold onto the tree limb above her.

The climbing man closed in enough to jump and grab the branch she was balancing on. His extra weight, combined with hers, served to bend the limb, and it slipped out from under her feet. Screaming, she clung to the tree branch and hung perilously in the air.

She heard the man on the ground laugh. "That's it, just shake her loose."

The climbing man answered, "We won't get no reward if she's dead."

"She's gonna wish she was dead anyway when I get done with her," the other stated and taunted her with graphic threats.

Abruptly, the ranting of the injured man stopped. The man in the tree noticed the sudden silence and took his hatchet from his belt. He yelled down, "I can easily kill her from here."

Alexandra had also noticed the sudden quiet and she was relieved to see the McGregor had finally made an appearance. Her hands were numb from holding onto the wet, snow-covered branch. She feared she would fall at any moment.

"So go ahead and kill her. The woman means nothing to me. I've only just met her," she heard the McGregor say. "You kill her, and then I'll kill you and go about my merry way."

Alexandra couldn't believe what she was hearing. *That scoundrel!*

Several seconds passed and the McGregor added, "Or you could help the lady down, and I'll let you live to take a message back to your Sullivan laird. The choice is yours."

The man didn't have to think long. He released the branch he'd pulled out from under her and sheathed his hatchet. He yelled down, "I'll take the message."

The branch did not spring all the way back up and Alexandra's toes barely reached it. She inched along until she was closer to the base of the tree, and then she stopped and leaned against the trunk, taking a minute to gain her composure. The climbing man moved down several more branches to give her room to descend. She was tempted to stay in the tree. She wasn't sure either man could be trusted. But she didn't have much of a choice, and she slowly made her way back down. The man remained close enough to help her should she start to slip or fall, and offered assistance along the way.

Her legs trembled by the time she finally stood on solid ground. Without looking directly at her, the McGregor ordered, "Wait here." He led the Sullivan man out of hearing distance and stood with his back toward her. As they spoke, she saw the man nod his head several times before he mounted his horse and rode away.

The McGregor glared as he strode back. She lifted her chin and glared right back at him. When he got close enough to reach her, his hands snaked out, and he grabbed her upper arms and pulled her abruptly against his chest. Startled, she looked up at him with her mouth open to protest. He brought his face down within inches of hers and said in a whisper, "The next time I tell you to do something"—and the whisper escalated to a roar—"by God, you better do it!" He gave her an extra little shake, before pushing her away.

Stunned, she yelled back, "You're mad at me? I came back to help you, you idiot!"

The McGregor pounded his massive chest with a fist, emphasizing each syllable as he yelled, "Do. I. Look. Like. I. Need. Help? Especially from a woman?"

Alexandra stared up into his angry face. *Actually, no, he didn't look like he needed anyone's assistance. He looked like a giant, a fierce warrior.* She took a deep breath and talked calmly to ease the building tension between them, "You may not have needed my help, but I *did* help. Next time, I'll leave you to your own devices."

"What you *did*, was almost get me killed!" He glanced down at his bleeding arm.

Alexandra hadn't noticed until then. Blood dripped from the fingertips of his left hand. She gasped and stated the obvious, "You're injured!" Stepping forward, she gently lifted his arm and examined the wound. Luckily, it wasn't as deep as she'd first feared.

"This should be cleaned and stitched right away."

The McGregor looked down with annoyance. "It can wait, we are only hours from the keep, and there are undoubtedly other bands of Sullivan's men nearby."

"You could lose your arm if it gets infected. At least let me apply a salve and a wrap. It will only take a few minutes." As she spoke, Alexandra ran in the direction of her horse. The McGregor didn't give her an answer, but he did follow. Thankfully, the animal was well trained and had not strayed far.

Ian sat in silence while she applied a paste she mixed from herbs and water. She had just enough clean wrapping material left to cover his muscular arm. She looked up into his brown eyes and found them already focused on her face. "That should hold until we reach your home. I'll stitch it for you then."

Ian nodded. "Let's get moving."

After retrieving his horse, they once again ventured out into the meadow, only this time they stayed close to the tree line and galloped across the remaining distance. The horses had rested during the skirmish so the McGregor pushed them at a faster pace. They rode for over an hour without speaking. Neither was in a talkative mood.

Alexandra thought back to the tree incident. The McGregor had stated so coldly she meant nothing to him. He had practically invited the Sullivan man to kill her. She couldn't help but wonder if that was how he really felt, even though he had followed up with a solution where no one was injured. She couldn't believe she was actually hurt by his comment. Personally, she thought a bond had formed between them during the time they'd been fighting for their lives. The more she thought about it, the more hurt and angry she became until she couldn't hold it back any longer.

"So…" She spoke loudly to get his attention, "You only just met me, and you wouldn't have cared if Sullivan's man did you a favor and got rid of me?"

The McGregor, taken aback by the tone and look upon her face, laughed out loud.

She didn't think it was funny and glared at him, which only served to make him laugh harder. When he caught his breath, he said, "Lass, the only thing I could do from the ground was to try to catch you, should you fall. There were far too many branches between him and me to deflect any weapon I threw. Sullivan's man was no fool. He knew what his fate would have been."

His response calmed her a little, and she even managed a wry smile at how ridiculous she must have looked, hanging high from the tree branch.

The sun reached midpoint when the McGregor stopped his horse and said, "We're getting closer to the stronghold. I don't think any of Sullivan's men will be foolish enough to venture this close."

He threw back his head and howled. Alexandra looked at him like he was crazy. What on earth was he doing? The pup jerked awake in the pouch, and he stuck his head out, his ears up and alert. The McGregor sat on his horse and listened for a few seconds before letting out another loud, drawn-out howl. Happy tilted his head back and joined in, howling mournfully. Alexandra smiled at his unexpected response. Perplexed, she watched the howling match before other answering howls coming from the surrounding woods startled her.

Her heart pounded, and she clutched the pup closer to her. Fearful of an oncoming attack, she glanced to the McGregor for a clue as what to do while she peered into the trees around them. The McGregor didn't appear disturbed. With a grin on his face, he jumped down from his horse as a group of men rode out of the woods and into the open. It took her a moment to realize they were also wearing the McGregor colors.

The men dismounted. Laughing and joking, they surrounded Ian and took turns shaking his hand or slapping him on the back. It was obvious he was well liked among his clansmen. They looked at her and the pup with open curiosity but stood back respectfully and waited for Ian to introduce her.

"Instead of explaining my tale over and over again,

I'll wait until everyone's gathered back at the main hall," he announced and mounted his horse.

The group surrounded them, forming a protective ring, as they walked their horses toward the McGregor keep. Alexandra's stomach fluttered with nerves about the upcoming encounter with the McGregor laird. Would he help her? Would Ian help plead her case? From what she could see so far, these men seemed to be a rather decent sort, which spoke well of their leader, didn't it?

The McGregor stronghold appeared in the distance. The stone fortress was tall, and intimidating, and it was surrounded by a stone wall. As they drew closer, they came upon clusters of huts at the base of the wall, near the gated entrance of the keep. From the huts, more and more people joined their procession. They were smiling and happy, yelling out to the McGregor and the other riders. Before long, a chant started. At first she couldn't make out what the people were saying, but as their voices grew stronger, she heard, "Wolf! Wolf! Wolf!" Alexandra held the pup closer to her chest. Many curious eyes were upon her and Happy. Why were they yelling Wolf? Was her pup in danger?

Passing through the outer wall of the keep, they entered the stables. The McGregor and the other riders dismounted, so she did also. She was glad to stand on ground once more. Young lads came forth from the stable and took their reins. Alexandra grabbed her medicinal bags before her horse could be led away. The McGregor seemed to have forgotten about her, as he was greeted by more and more people. He loudly made the announcement for everyone to come into the main hall. Alexandra trailed behind but stayed as close to him as she could.

As forbidding as the outside of the stronghold was, the inside was the complete opposite. The hall was clean and bright, warm and inviting. Tapestries hung from the walls and fires blazed from multiple fireplaces. The McGregor was loudly greeted and given a bear hug from a large man whom Alexandra assumed to be his brother, as the man looked like a younger, slightly smaller version of Ian. Alexandra's eyes searched the growing crowd for a glimpse of the McGregor laird. Ian raised his hands to silence the people.

"I was delayed returning from my hunt due to being captured by Sullivan and his men," Ian shouted so all could hear. Silence prevailed as his words sank in, and then the crowd erupted with yelling and curses toward the Sullivan clan. Ian held up his hand again to quiet them so he could continue.

"Sullivan took me to the Englishman, Niles Conrad, at whose estate I was kept prisoner." He raised his fist in the air and shouted, "They are in league to overtake our lands!"

The people exploded again but silenced themselves as he added, "They had no idea I was the McGregor laird, and they only kept me alive to try to torture information from me about our fortress and defenses. But as you can see, I escaped *and* I have brought with me Sullivan's bride-to-be as my prisoner!"

Cheering interrupted any further talk, and weapons were raised overhead as the chanting of "Wolf" started all over again.

Blood drained from Alexandra's face as the McGregor's words fully sank in. Everything suddenly became crystal clear and she remembered Aggie's statement that the clan was headed by a man nicknamed "the Wolf".

She slowly set the pup on the ground. As the crowd cheered and stared, something inside her exploded. Before she had time to gain control, she leapt across the few feet that separated her from the McGregor and flung herself at him.

Chapter Six

"Liar! Scoundrel!" she yelled, pummeling his chest and face as hard as she could with her fists.

Multiple gasps sounded and then complete silence enveloped the room as the crowd waited in shock for the Wolf's retribution. James McGregor pulled out a dagger and stepped forward to pull the wild banshee off his brother. Ian shook his head and laughingly picked Alexandra up and tossed her over his shoulder. She continued to pound him with her fists and call him every bad name she could remember having heard. The McGregor's laughter infuriated her further, and she bit him through his clothing.

Feeling the pinch of her teeth, Ian slapped her bottom hard and walked to the staircase leading to the bedrooms. The silence of the crowd slowly turned to laughter and ribald remarks as the McGregor carried her up the steps with the wolf pup following at his feet.

At the top of the stairway, he paused at the first doorway on his right. With one hand braced against her bottom, he used the other to open the door. Stepping in, he held the door until the pup crossed the threshold. He walked to the large, oversized bed and using both hands, tossed Alexandra upon it. She pushed off to come at him again. Grasping both fists in one hand, the McGregor backed her up against the edge of the bed until she lost her balance and landed down on it, following with his own weight. He held her hands over her head and straddled her body, wrapping his legs around hers to keep her from kicking and bucking.

Alexandra struggled in vain for several more minutes before the fight drained out of her. She was embarrassed when her anger dissolved to tears. She moved her head to the side, refusing to look at the McGregor's face which loomed above her.

"I didna lie to you," Ian whispered, "I told you my real name, lass."

She turned and glared at him through her tears. "You also said you were a guard."

"I am the guard of my people and land." He smiled a rakish smile and then said, "No harm will come to you. You'll like being my prisoner, I promise."

Prisoner. The word reverberated in her head. She couldn't keep the tears at bay, and she cried wretchedly, as she had not cried since she was a child.

****

Ian left her crying on the bed. He scooped up the whining wolf pup on his way out. He had expected her surprise and anger when he revealed his identity, and he had looked forward with anticipation to their verbal sparring, but he was totally unprepared for her heartbreaking tears.

The crowd below had dispersed and only his brother and his warriors remained. He approached the long table where they sat talking among themselves and ordered two of his men to guard the door to his bedroom. Addressing his warriors, he said, "I want her watched by two at all times. She is free to roam the keep as long as she is guarded. Don't be fooled. She is very crafty."

Turning to his brother, he held the wolf pup higher. "Can you let it be known to all that no harm is to come to this wolf or to the woman?"

James nodded his agreement. "Where did you get the little devil?"

"She found him and has been mothering him." Ian sat the pup down and let him loose. Happy circled the table and cautiously sniffed each man before coming back to sit at Ian's feet.

"Do you want me to send a ransom note to Sullivan?" James asked.

"Aye. Make it for an exorbitant amount. Send one to Conrad also. Let them stew a bit. We'll go to war with them after spring breaks."

James grinned at the bloodlust in his tone. "It's good to have you back, brother."

****

Alexandra cried until her throat burned and she had no tears left. Totally exhausted, she lay upon the fur-covered bed and stared at the ceiling. She had always been so calm and in control of her emotions, necessary for survival when living with Niles. The McGregor had turned her into a screaming, raging shrew. She was so embarrassed. How had she let him get under her skin? Thinking of his betrayal, her eyes burned once more. What a fool she'd been. She began to pray. "Dear Lord, first of all, please forgive me for my lack of control, for striking out in anger and setting such a bad example for a Christian woman. Please help me to forgive that black-hearted McGregor!" Feeling anger swell, she changed the subject. "Lord, please take me back to the abbey where I can be in peace and live to worship You." She prayed where her thoughts led her until she ran out of words.

She rose from the bed and went to stand by the one window in the room. Looking down, she saw the distance to the ground was far too great to attempt an escape. Even if she could manage such a feat, there were too many people around to witness it. To the right, she observed the defensive stone wall and the guarded gate, and to the left, more huts lined the inner wall.

A timid knock interrupted her thoughts. Seconds after, the door opened wide enough for a red-headed girl to stick her head through. The young girl met her eyes briefly, and she shyly entered the room.

"My laird has ordered a bath for you," she said and turned to hold the door open for two servants to carry in a large copper tub. Those two servants were followed in by several more, all of whom carried steaming pots of water.

Alexandra was tempted to have the girl tell her laird she didn't want any favors. However, the thought of a long soak and feeling clean again was too much of an enticement to turn down.

"We have many pots on the fire. It shouldn't take too long to fill your bath." The girl avoided making direct eye contact and fidgeted with her apron. She cleared her throat and asked, "Do you have any clean clothes?"

"Yes, in my bags." Alexandra answered and glanced around the room before she remembered having dropped them on the main hall floor before she'd set down the pup. The pup. "Where is my wolf pup?" she asked.

"He is with the laird. Orders have been given that no harm is to come to him. Don't worry, no one would think of crossing the Wolf." Alexandra noticed her dimples when she smiled. She was striking looking with wild, curly red hair and a splatter of freckles over her nose and cheeks.

"What is your name?" Alexandra asked returning the girl's smile. "And how old are you?"

"I'm Maddie, and I've just turned fifteen."

"Maddie, I am very happy to meet you, though I wish it were under better circumstances. I hope we can be friends."

The girl beamed and gave a quick curtsy. "I'll bring up your bags," she said and disappeared out the door. While the girl was away, Alexandra took the opportunity to hide the dagger she kept at her ankle. Looking about the room and not finding a good hiding place to conceal it, she settled for tucking the blade under the edge of the fur that topped the bed. She'd put it back on just as soon as she donned clean clothes.

Pots of steaming water were dumped until the tub was three-quarters full. Alexandra investigated and discovered a lock on the inside of the bedroom chamber door. She engaged it before letting Maddie help her disrobe. She gasped as she climbed into the tub and eased herself down into the water. The water was so hot. Blessedly hot. She leaned back and shut her eyes, letting the warmth seep in. Maddie helped undo her messy braid and started combing through her hair. She never wanted to get out of this tub. As her aching muscles relaxed, she washed her hair several times until it was squeaky clean.

The water started to cool, and she was considering getting out of the tub when the bedroom door handle shook. A loud knock followed. Alexandra sat up so abruptly that water splashed over the sides of the tub.

"Don't let anyone in!"

Maddie stopped in the midst of combing out her hair. "Yes?" she asked, raising her voice to be heard through the door.

"Is she still in the tub?" Alexandra heard the McGregor ask.

"Aye," Maddie replied.

"Tell her to save me some hot water. She's got five minutes, and then I'm coming in."

Alexandra stood up in the tub and reached for the soft cloth Maddie handed her. Wrapping it around her top half, she hurried to get out and start drying off. She didn't trust the McGregor to wait five minutes. She asked the girl to pull her spare dress from one of the bags. The material was extremely wrinkled, but at least it was clean. Maddie handed her clean undergarments and assisted Alexandra in pulling the dress over her head.

Assuming the McGregor would break the door if it was still locked when he came back, Alexandra went ahead and undid the bolt. Chances were, she'd want to be able to lock it again at another time. She pulled a chair close to the fire and sat while Maddie worked on untangling the knots from her hair. Minutes later, the McGregor strode in without bothering to knock. Several servants followed carrying more pots of hot water. He nodded to Maddie and said, "Thank you" in a dismissive tone. Maddie handed Alexandra the comb and quickly exited the room. Alexandra ignored the laird's presence and combed her hair, letting it dry before the fire.

She sat stiffly and did not look in his direction. The

McGregor began to undress. Taking his time, he drew out the process.

Had the man no shame? Wasn't he going to send her from the room? Though he wasn't standing directly in front of her, she clearly saw him from the side. She could feel her cheeks grow warmer as she tried to keep her attention on the fire. Her breath caught. He had a magnificent body. Finally, he sat down in the tub, and Alexandra found herself able to breathe again. She heard splashing and a groan before he fell silent. Turning her head slightly, she gave a quick glance. His head was tilted back, and his eyes were shut.

The tub looked ridiculously small with him in it. His injured arm was wrapped in a different colored cloth than the one she had used. She could only assume someone else had stitched him up. Too bad, she thought, she would have enjoyed pricking his skin. Anger rose up in her. Taking deep, slow breaths, she returned her gaze to the fire. What she needed to do now was to make a plan. She knew no one, and she was totally unfamiliar with the land. She'd just have to be alert and wait for an opportunity to present itself.

"Woman, there'll be no getting away from me, so put your mind at ease," the McGregor said, almost as if he'd read her mind. She met his intense gaze with a blank stare but said nothing.

"As long as you do as I say, you'll be treated kindly." He paused, but she refrained from making a retort.

"And I'm sure it'll take plenty of time for Sullivan and your cousin to come up with the hefty ransom I'm asking," he added.

Feeling her anger rise again, she glared at him but

refused to respond to his prodding. He smiled and stood without warning. She gasped as her eyes dropped of their own accord to his private parts. Averting her head quickly, her cheeks flushed.

"You are free to walk about the keep, but you'll have guards at all times," he said to her back as he dressed.

Alexandra felt an immediate sense of relief at his words. "And where am I to sleep?" she asked and turned to face him.

"Here in this chamber with me. You may sleep in my bed or make yourself one on the floor. The decision is entirely yours, but you'll stay with me during the night hours." Ian sat on the edge of the bed and stomped into his boots.

"I'm sure I'll be comfortable on the floor," she said through gritted teeth and turned back to face the fireplace once more.

"I'll send Maddie for you when it's time for dinner," he said over his shoulder and walked out of the room.

Alexandra stood up the minute he left. Pacing back and forth, she evaluated her situation. At least she was free to roam the keep. That would open up more opportunities for escape. Drat the man for insisting she sleep in his chamber. Obviously, he didn't trust her, which was wise on his part. All things considered, she was still better off than she was in Niles's hands. By the time Niles sent the ransom, if he even did, she would have formed more of a plan.

When Maddie came back to announce it was time to go down to dinner, Alexandra was in better spirits. She would make it through this trial. After having time to think about it, she realized more than anything, her anger was due to the pain of being betrayed. And she probably wouldn't feel so hurt if she had not developed feelings for the McGregor. She didn't understand these feelings or why she felt a bond with the man, but obviously they were one-sided feelings that she would just have to squelch.

Maddie and Alexandra walked down the staircase together. The wolf pup noticed her first and yipped with excitement. He raced up the staircase to meet her. He jumped up on her skirts so she reached down and picked him up, holding him close. The talk around the tables tapered to silence and people stared. Some looks were curious, while others were openly hostile. Ian stood and pulled out the chair next to him. With as much dignity and grace as she could muster, she made her way to the table. The last time these people had seen her, she had screamed obscenities and attacked their laird. How could she dispel that impression?

The McGregor stood until she was seated and then poured her a glass of red wine. Food was passed and the talking resumed. Alexandra set the pup on the floor between them and intermittently fed him scraps of meat. She looked around the long tables and listened to the sounds of talking and laughter. The men appeared to be the McGregor warriors, and the women who were present with some of them, she presumed to be their wives. One woman in particular stood out. She had auburn hair and her dress was cut so low Alexandra feared her large breasts would tumble out. Seated at the far end of her table, the woman stared at Alexandra with open hatred. Their eyes connected briefly before the woman turned and leaned into her male companion, whispering something in his ear. They both threw back their heads in laughter.

The McGregor drew her attention and introduced her to his brother James, seated across from him and to James's young son, Jamie, who sat next to his father. She nodded and received a curt nod in return. She sensed hostility from James and even from his son, who could be no more than four or five, but who managed to glare at her quite nicely. She wondered what the father had said about her that the child had picked up on. The boy was precocious. He had the dark features of his father and uncle, combined with the face of an angel. Jamie might not like her, but he was smitten by the pup. He leaned down to peer under the table and throw bits of food in the pup's direction until his father admonished him to sit up and eat. Where was his mother? Had something happened to her?

The McGregor proved to be a good host, inquiring if she had found enough to eat and keeping her wine glass full. She was surprised to be treated so well, but remained wary. She did not initiate conversation with the McGregor but answered his questions politely. James told his older brother of the news he had missed during his three week absence, which included the death of someone's cow and a fistfight between two of his men over one of the cook's daughters. It was evident to Alexandra as she listened to the tales that the McGregor brothers cared about all the members of their clan.

With her stomach full of food and wine, her eyelids grew heavy. What a day it had been. She was unbelievably tired. Talk around the table droned on. Afraid that she would embarrass herself further by falling asleep, she waited for a pause in the conversation and asked the McGregor if she could be excused. His dark eyes met hers, and he gestured for Maddie. Thankfully, her exit from the dining hall went relatively unnoticed in comparison to her entrance.

****

"Bitch," the woman known as Debra muttered under her breath, staring daggers into the back of the blonde English woman leaving the hall. She saw the way the Wolf watched the blonde whore. The Wolf was hers! She'd plotted to gain the brothers' attention since she moved into the clan as Robert's woman.

Spotting an opportunity, she rose and placed her hand on Robert's shoulder. "I'm going to help serve."

He patted her hand in acknowledgment and kept talking to his friend. She sashayed to the end of the table and picked up the empty wine bottle in front of the brothers.

"Would my laird like more wine?" She leaned and stretched across the table, bending low at the waist to give them an ample view of her bosom as she reached for the Englishwoman's empty glass, plate and napkin.

"No thank you." The McGregor pushed his empty goblet and plate toward her.

"It is good to have you back." She smiled her sweetest.

The laird nodded but didn't interrupt his brother's talk to answer.

She turned with her hands full and let go of the napkin, bending low again and pushing her derriere out as she bent to pick it up. Glancing back as she stood, she saw they were still locked in conversation.

She strode toward the kitchen, frustrated at their

lack of interest. The brothers should have taken notice of her by now. She laughed and openly flirted when Robert wasn't around. She looked for every opportunity to run into one of them alone outside the keep. So far, she'd not had any luck.

Perhaps they were reserved because she was spoken for as Robert's woman. Clan honor and all that nonsense. Maybe she should break it off with Robert, but she had no means of supporting herself. She'd be expected to return to her clan in the lowlands. Unless she latched onto another warrior, but that wouldn't do her any good.

Debra threw her handful of dishes into the washtub without scraping them off, earning a dirty look from the kitchen help.

What if an accident claimed Robert's life? She'd be overcome with grief. Certainly they'd feel obliged to help her. If she could just get the Wolf drunk and alone, she was sure he'd fall under her seductive spell. But now this Englishwoman had arrived. She was going to ruin everything.

Chapter Seven

When Alexandra reached the McGregor's bedroom, she turned to the two guards who had followed her. "I'm sorry you're missing out on the rest of the festivities." They did not acknowledge her apology but rather took up their posts on either side of the doorway. Maddie entered the room behind her. Normally, she would have no problem getting herself ready for bed, but tonight she was grateful for Maddie's assistance. The girl brought her a soft, flannel gown which covered her from head to toe. Extra blankets had also been placed near the fire hearth. She thanked Maddie and ushered her out of the room so her new friend could go back and join the others in the dining hall.

The fire was warm and inviting, and so were her blankets from being so close to the heat. She was asleep within seconds of slipping into the makeshift bed. During what she presumed to be the middle of the night, she woke up to a very cold, very dark room. Her hip and elbow ached from lying on one side for too long on the hard, stone floor. As she lay shivering, she heard the rustle of the straw mattress followed by soft snoring. She must have slept like the dead not to have heard the McGregor come into the room. The fire was completely out. Had the McGregor stoked it before he retired? She doubted she would have slept through that since she was only a few feet from the hearth. Perhaps that was why he had not stoked it—because she was sleeping? Ha, she thought, unwilling to give him any credit. He was probably drunk from too much wine and had just stumbled into bed.

The night stretched endlessly long. She rolled from side to side as her discomfort with the hard floor grew. The blankets shifted and twisted into lumps. Curling into a ball and tucking the blankets close, was the best she could do to keep warm. Unfortunately, her hip and elbow would start throbbing, and she'd roll over and start the whole process again.

Alexandra listened to the McGregor snoring intermittently throughout the night. She was tempted during those times to crawl into the other side of the large bed. He probably wouldn't even notice, and she could get up again before dawn. He'd never know. She snorted and thought, *like I could trust myself to wake up and not be in his warm arms again*. Just thinking about his hard body wrapped around her, made her feel warmer. She couldn't risk it. She was too attracted to him to let her defenses down.

She feigned sleep when morning finally came and the McGregor moved about his quarters. After he stomped into his boots and left the room, she got up from the floor and stretched her sore muscles before jumping into the big bed. The blankets were still warm from his body heat. Pulling the big top fur over her head, she snuggled into the sagging softness. She was pleasantly drifting off to sleep when the bedroom door crashed open and she heard the McGregor shout, "Wake-up, you lazy lass. There's work to be done!"

Alexandra sat up as the McGregor pulled the

covers off the bed. He stared at her uncovered legs before she jumped to her feet.

"Everyone pulls their weight around here, and that includes you." He stood with his feet spread and his hands on his hips.

Alexandra glared at him. "I've no problem doing my fair share! You could have told me what you expected last night so I could be ready for whatever menial task you have in mind."

The McGregor's dark eyes were dancing. *Was he laughing at her?*

"Our clan healer is sick, and you could make yourself useful by checking on him."

Alexandra's anger dissipated at the news. "I will gladly help if I can. Give me a few minutes to get myself and my supplies together."

"Maddie is on her way with your breakfast. Whenever you are ready, your guards can show you the way to the healer's hut." He walked toward the door, and then turned back.

"I've given young Jamie the task of looking after your pup until you return." He watched her as if gauging her reaction.

"Thank you. I'm sure that Happy will enjoy the lad's attention."

The McGregor smirked at the mention of the pup's name and left the room.

****

Alexandra's guards this morning were Brock and Sean. Both had been reluctant to divulge their names until she said she wouldn't go anywhere with them until they did. If she was going to be stuck here for a time, than she was going to get acquainted with these people.

Besides, being on a first name basis with her guards might eventually help her to escape.

The healer's hut turned out to be one of the buildings inside the keep's fortress wall, and the walk to it was a short and easy one as the snow had been trampled by many footsteps. She knocked on the hut door, but there was no response. She looked back at her captors, who both nodded as she opened the door. The interior was dark, damp, and cold. She could make out a bed and walked over to it. The occupant was unresponsive, and he was straining to breathe. Placing her hand upon his brow, she discovered he was burning with fever.

Alexandra shrugged out of her fur cloak and laid it over the man's bedcovers. She turned to Brock and Sean, "Can one of you please start a fire? And the other bring a good supply of fresh water." As the men did as she bade, she rolled up her sleeves and looked about the room for items she needed.

Within the hour, a steady fire burned in the fireplace, and Alexandra had several brews simmering in adjacent cook pots. She stripped the poor man's bed as it was soaked in sweat, and she placed cool rags over his body in an attempt to lower his fever. Brock assisted in propping the healer into a half-reclining position. She held a bowl of foul-smelling brew beneath the healer's chin and pulled her cloak up and over both their heads so she could see to feed him. The trapped steam from the bowl would help open his airway. After a time, she noted his breathing eased a bit. Removing the cloak, she talked to her patient and encouraged him to clear his lungs by spitting up phlegm when he could.

She asked a guard to fetch a bowl of the next brew

and used a spoon to feed it to the sick man. It was a slow process, as she had to coax him to open his mouth and then to swallow. Alexandra continued the pattern over and over again. First she cooled his body with cold rags, tenting him so he could fully inhale the vapors, and then she spooned as much brew into him as he would take.

The hours flew by. She didn't stop to eat, although she made sure that her guards did. The poor man was hanging on by a thread. As she worked, she petitioned God to save his life. She didn't know what else to do for him.

Finally, a breakthrough appeared, and the healer, whose name she learned was Silas, became fully conscious. Conscious and cantankerous.

"Woman, leave me alone. Can't you let an old man die in peace?" he rasped and shoved the foul tasting brew aside.

"You are not going to die. Your clan needs you," she said and held another spoonful to the man's pursed lips, but he refused to open them.

"Then you take care of them," he spluttered as she slipped more brew into his open mouth.

"But I don't have your experience. In fact, I have very little. I'm going to need your expertise. You could teach me much before you leave this world." As she talked, she spooned brew into his mouth.

"Well, I do know a lot, and that's a fact," the old man said proudly.

"And I will be an eager student. But first we must get you back on your feet. You've almost finished the bowl, just a few more swallows." She cajoled the man into taking a few more sips. Placing her hand on his forehead, she was pleased to note the fever was indeed going down.

Nighttime came, and her guards were replaced with new ones. She was too busy and too tired to bother asking their names, but they readily assisted her.

After several more hours passed, Maddie appeared at the hut entrance. "The laird has sent me to tell you and the guards it is time to come back to the keep."

Alexandra did not move from the healer's bedside. "You may tell the McGregor that I'm not ready to leave. However, his guards may leave at any time."

The guards and Maddie exchanged worried glances. It was not difficult for Alexandra to understand their dilemma. The guards had been ordered not to leave her unattended, but if they had to carry her back kicking and screaming, what would the Wolf's reaction be? And Maddie was so bashful she was probably scared to tell the laird that she had said no.

Alexandra sighed and said, "Simply tell the McGregor I regret I must decline his offer. His healer still needs attention. You may also tell him his dutiful guards could not abandon their post. He won't be angry with *you*."

The girl hesitated a moment before concluding she had no other option. She nodded and turned away.

Within minutes, the McGregor's large form filled the healer's doorway. With his arms folded, he lounged against the doorframe.

"You have two choices. You can walk back with me, or I'll carry you."

Alexandra opened her mouth to protest but was cut short when he interrupted, "I also value my healer's life. If you get sick you'll be of no help to him. Your guards have been watching. They can take over for the night."

She knew he would make good on this threat and she did not wish to make a spectacle of herself again in front of his clan. She turned her back to him and gave instructions to the guards. Putting on her cloak, she side-stepped past the McGregor.

The walk to the keep was a quiet one. He guided her through the darkness with his hand at her elbow. Several groups of people still lounged at the tables when they entered the hall. Alexandra went straight up the stairs to the bedroom. She was relieved the McGregor did not follow. She was so exhausted she felt sick. Changing into her nightgown, she let her clothes lie where they fell and climbed into the pallet of blankets on the floor. Her last thought before she fell asleep was surprise that the floor was quite comfortable.

****

The McGregor found Alexandra fast asleep on the hearth when he entered his bedchamber. He stoked the fire for the evening, but even that did not wake her. Deciding he'd had enough of her stubbornness for one day, he lifted her gently from the floor and placed her on the bed. She muttered in her sleep and rolled over on her side, curling into a fetal position. He stared down at her. Admiring her pale, flawless skin, he touched the smoothness of her cheek before picking up a lock of her silky hair and running it between his fingertips. He smiled at the memory of her brushing her long tresses with her back stiff and facing the fire while he bathed, and again, when he remembered how wild and untamed it had looked around her face when he'd jolted her awake that morning. He held back a laugh as he thought of the look on her face when he'd risen from the tub. God, he enjoyed teasing this lass. Drawing his hand back, he covered her with blankets and furs and retreated to the far side of the bed.

The morning rays streaked through his bedroom window before the McGregor woke. To his surprise, Alexandra lay in his arms. Her legs entwined with his, her arms encircled him and her head rested upon his chest. With one arm wrapped around her back and the other under her derriere, he slid her completely on top his chest and hips. She stirred a bit and then molded herself more completely against him. With the palms of his hands he softly stroked her back while his lips nuzzled her neck.

****

Alexandra was having the most wondrous dream. She was warm and cozy. In her dream Ian McGregor was smiling into her eyes and he was tenderly kissing her lips. He wrapped his arms around her and deepened the kiss, touching and caressing her tongue with his. Hands gripped her hips and pulled her tight against his loins. She could feel the hard ridge of his shaft as it pressed against her.

Intense pleasure brought her out of her slumber. She opened her eyes and raised her head to find herself inches from the McGregor's face, his dark eyes staring deep into hers. It took her a few seconds to totally wake up and to realize she was lying *on top* of the McGregor. With a yelp, she tried to throw her body to the side, but the McGregor was quicker. He turned with her in his arms and suddenly she found herself trapped beneath him.

"Oh no, you don't," he said, "you started this and I'm not ready to stop." He grabbed her hands and held them over her head.

Alexandra was speechless. Had she started it? When had she climbed into bed?

The McGregor took advantage of her hesitation and brought his lips down to hers again. The kiss was powerful. He gently ravished her mouth, stroking and sucking until she couldn't help but respond. Tentatively, she touched his tongue with hers and began to return the strokes. He released her hands and she wrapped them around his back, holding him close. As he kissed her, he moved a hand to her breast, stroking the nipple through the flannel gown. He released her lips to suckle the hidden bud. Fire coursed through her and she arched her back to bring the nipple closer to him. She felt the firm ridge of his loins as he pressed her harder into the bed. She was suddenly overwhelmed by feelings of need and want. She never could have imagined feeling this way. Fighting her own desire, she turned her head to the side and pushed against his chest.

"Please stop," she said.

The McGregor turned his attention to her neck, gently nibbling below her ear.

"Is it your intention to take me against my will?"

He lifted his head and turned her face back to his. Looking for confirmation in her eyes, he said, "We both know it wouldn't be against your will."

Shamed, her eyes filled with tears. "So you would defile me and ruin my reputation?"

"Woman, you sleep in my chamber. Don't you think people already believe us to be lovers?"

"*I* know the truth. And any future husband will

know the truth," she said.

"Have you forgotten your betrothed is the Sullivan? Do you really want your first time to be with him?"

Alexandra glared at him through her tears and resisted the urge to punch him in the face. "What I want is to be left alone by *all* men and to go back to the abbey."

The McGregor returned her angry look and released her to roll off the bed. She averted her eyes as he dressed and left the room.

What had she gotten herself into?

Chapter Eight

Alexandra did her best to stay out of the McGregor's way. The next couple of weeks passed slowly. She continued to nurse the healer Silas back to health, and his improvement increased each day. On her walks to and from the keep, she usually saw the McGregor and his brother James from a distance on the training field with their men. From what she'd observed, it looked like each brother trained his own men, and then they competed one on one, or group on group.

The McGregor demanded she attend the evening meals, and not wanting to cause further tension, she complied. Though they sat next to one another, neither started conversation. She slept on the floor in his bed chamber but made sure to retire before he did and waited until he left the room each morning before getting up. After several days, she admitted to herself she missed his teasing banter.

The wolf pup greeted her with exuberance each morning after having spent the night sleeping with young Jamie. The boy had warmed to her, and she attributed it to their shared affection for Happy. Every day, he was eager to show her new tricks he had taught the wolf. The lad, as young as he was, appeared to have free rein of the keep without the constant supervision of a nanny. Most times, he tagged along behind her and the guards, and he chattered nonstop about the pup.

Today, as Alexandra stepped out of the keep, she was pleased to find the weather considerably warmer than usual. She hoped it was a sign spring would arrive soon. The day was a beautiful reprieve from the harsh winter. The snow slushed beneath her feet, and water dripped continuously as it melted from overhead tree branches. When her entourage passed by the training field, Alexandra automatically slowed her pace to watch the McGregor spar with his brother. She had been surprised to learn the McGregor and his clansmen trained for hours every day, no matter the weather. Undoubtedly, they were preparing for battle with her cousin and the Sullivan.

****

Ian spotted Alexandra the minute she stepped out from the keep. She was like a ray of sunshine. Everyone was drawn to her warmth. Even his guards had fallen under her spell, and quarrels ensued over whose turn it was to stand watch. Today, his besotted nephew also trotted after her with the wolf pup in tow. With his mind on the woman, it was easy for his brother to dislodge his sword from his hand and put his own at Ian's throat.

"You've let that woman get under your skin, haven't you, brother?" he asked. "What do you plan on doing with her? Don't forget she's English."

"She may be English, but she has a good heart. I'll rot in hell before I let the Sullivan pig get his hands on her." Ian picked up his fallen sword and turned his back toward the lady in question. Sparring more aggressively, he backed his brother away.

****

87

Alexandra hadn't realized she'd come to a complete stop until little Jamie asked where they were going.

"We're off to see Silas again this morning. But first, I think we should take advantage of the nice weather and take a walk around the lake. Would you like that?"

"Yes!" he shouted and ran toward the lake followed by the excited pup.

Alexandra laughed. She didn't blame them as she felt the same way. She was tired of being stuck indoors. The frozen lake was in plain sight of the keep walls and the guards who stood watch on them, so her personal guards did not try to dissuade her. Jamie ran and threw sticks for the pup to fetch. Running ahead, the boy yelled back at her to hurry up. Growing warm, she took off her fur cloak and decided to carry it for a while.

She was familiar with all of her guards' names. After initially forcing conversation on them, she now also knew their family names and had even treated some of them. Although they weren't as stiff and formal as they had been, they still kept a pretty watchful eye over her. Today, they gave her a little more freedom and privacy by allowing her and the boy to walk ahead.

Jamie threw a large stick out onto the icy lake and laughed as the pup slipped and slid to retrieve it. Alexandra chuckled at the sight of Happy with his legs splayed out in every direction and his body spinning in circles. She stopped walking for a moment and lifted her face up to the sun, enjoying the warmth and peace of the day.

She heard the pup's yelp at the same time she

heard the boy cry out. Jamie had tossed the stick close to a large hole in the ice and Happy had slid into the freezing water. Jamie ran out onto the ice to help the pup. Both Alexandra and the guards yelled for the boy to stop, but he didn't listen. As he reached the edge of the hole, the ice broke, sending Jamie splashing into the lake.

Alexandra ran onto the ice with the guards not too far behind. The ice creaked and cracked, and she yelled over her shoulder for the guards to stay back or they would all end up in the lake. She hurried as close to the hole as she dared. She heard ice splinter as she lay down and stretched her arm to Jamie. His arms flailed about as he tried to grasp hold of the pup. Throwing her cloak out toward the boy, she screamed for him to grab it.

"Jamie! You *cannot* save that pup until you save yourself!"

Finally her words sank in, and the lad grabbed her cloak. As she pulled, he lifted the top half of his body out of the hole. Holding the cloak with one hand, he reached back and grabbed the pup by the scruff of its neck.

Alexandra rose to her hands and knees and backed up as quickly as she could until the guards grabbed her ankles and pulled her and the boy to safety.

She clutched Jamie to her and reverently thanked God for his safety. The boy was already shivering and turning blue when she wrapped him in the fur cloak with the pup he refused to leave behind. She lifted him up to carry when one of the guards took him from her and started running toward the keep. The other guard assisted her in running as they followed close behind.

Before they had covered half the distance to the keep, the McGregor and his brother ran out to meet them. James grabbed his son from the guard and sprinted for the keep. The McGregor took the guard's place at her side.

"Are you all right?" he questioned, noting her wet clothing. "We heard the screams on the training field and saw what happened."

"Yes, but we need to get Jamie out of those wet clothes and warmed up immediately," she said breathlessly.

"James knows what to do. He will care for his son. You may check on him after you've changed out of your own wet clothing." Ian put his arm around her shoulders and escorted her back into the keep and up to his bed chamber, where he left her in Maddie's care.

Alexandra's teeth started chattering. In her worry over the boy, she hadn't realized how wet and cold she herself had become. The front of her gown was soaked and heavy against her skin. Maddie assisted her in removing each layer of clothing and wrapped her in a rough, wool blanket. No sooner had she covered her nakedness than the McGregor barged in holding a steaming mug.

"Drink this." He thrust the drink toward her.

Alexandra fought to keep the blanket in place. She freed one hand and clutched the covering closed with the other. Taking hold of the mug with a shaking hand, she brought it to her lips and took a little sip.

"Mmmm, not bad. What is this?" she asked and took another sip while waiting for his answer.

"Spiced ale. Drink it down while it's hot." The McGregor took her arm and led her to the chair in front of the fire. He pushed down on her shoulders to get her to sit. Popping right back up, she stated, "I want to see Jamie."

"Not until you finish the ale." He pushed her back down into the chair. "And get dressed in the dry clothes Maddie went to fetch."

As he said her name, Maddie entered carrying an array of clothing. Alexandra put the mug to her mouth and gulped down the entire contents in a very unladylike manner. Thankfully, the ale was not scorching hot, but instantly its warmth spread from within. She stood too quickly and stumbled over the blanket that had wrapped itself around her feet. The McGregor caught her by the shoulders and steadied her against his chest. Alexandra's cheeks flushed red as she was vividly aware of her nakedness beneath the blanket.

She stepped back and Ian released his hold on her. "I'll be waiting outside the door to escort you to Jamie."

She opened the bedroom door after dressing to find him leaning against the wall. Taking her elbow, he led the way through the halls until they reached the boy's room. They knocked and were summoned into the chamber. James sat in a chair drawn close to his son's bed. He held Jamie's hand between his and listened as the child heralded his adventure. At their approach, James looked up, acknowledging their presence before turning his attention back to his son.

Young Jamie lay under a mound of covers. His cheeks were flushed and his eyes were bright as he told of his near drowning. The boy's free hand was wrapped around the wolf pup, holding him close as if still in danger of losing him. Alexandra put her hand over his brow to gauge his temperature. She smiled with relief to find him without a fever.

The boy looked at her and said, "Isn't that right? You saved me and I saved Happy."

"You were the bravest little boy I've ever seen. Happy is lucky to have such a courageous friend."

James said, "My son was lucky you responded so quickly. I am in your debt. Thank you." He took her hand and kissed it.

Alexandra was surprised by his gesture. He had not been the friendliest of men up to this point.

The McGregor pulled her hand back from his brother's grasp and said, "I think that's enough thanks."

****

The incident with young Jamie that morning also broke the ice between her and the McGregor. After checking on Jamie's condition, Ian escorted her to the healer's hut before leaving her to practice with his men.

Several days earlier, Silas had insisted he was well enough to resume his duties, and they had begun to check on the health of his fellow clansmen. Alexandra enjoyed accompanying him every day as he went from home to home. She learned the name of everyone she met as well as their place within the clan. On the whole, she considered the clan to be very healthy. A few members had colds or slight fevers, but no one was critically ill.

They also examined several women in various stages of pregnancy, but Silas explained he did not actually deliver the babies as older women usually assisted the birthing mother; however, he was available for potions and brews to ease the expectant mother's pain. Today, as they finished up and headed back to Silas's hut, the McGregor himself came to relieve her guards and escort her back for dinner.

"Have you enjoyed your day?" he inquired as they walked back to the keep while the sun set.

"Yes, Silas is a very knowledgeable teacher, and I enjoy his company." Alexandra put the hood of her cloak up as the temperature dropped with the sun.

"So what do you think of my clansman?" he asked.

Alexandra was surprised, but she was glad he was talkative this evening. The tension of the past weeks had been hard to live with, and she was ready to call a truce.

"I think your people are strong and proud, and they are obviously very loyal to you." She paused before admitting, "You are a good leader."

The McGregor smiled and lifted his chin. "Of course I am."

They reached the hall, and he took their cloaks and handed them to a servant before he walked her to their place at the head table. His brother James and the warriors who usually sat with them were already present, and she was pleasantly surprised when they all rose from their seats as she approached. She looked at the McGregor who simply smiled and pulled out her chair. As she sat down, so did everyone else.

She looked at James and asked, "How is young Jamie doing?"

"Thank God there's still no fever, but he's not very happy that I've ordered him to stay in bed until tomorrow. This is not his first mishap. If I can just keep him alive until he's ten, he might live to reach adulthood," he replied.

"May I check in on him later?"

"I'm sure he'll enjoy your company," James said and poured her a glass of wine before handing the bottle to his brother.

Everyone appeared to be in especially good spirits that evening. Talking and laughter filled the hall and echoed against the stone walls. Alexandra felt more relaxed among the clan than she ever had before. She leaned back with her second glass of wine and watched the two brothers tease and torment one another until they were interrupted by one of the gate guardsman who came in from the cold and whispered something in the McGregor's ear. The laird's expression changed instantly to serious and he commanded, "Bring the man in."

Voices tapered off and silence ensued as a stranger was escorted before the McGregor. Alexandra thought she recognized the man as one of Niles's guardsmen, but she wasn't certain. The man was nervous, and he swallowed repeatedly. As he did so, his Adam's apple bobbed up and down. She couldn't blame him for being scared with the way everyone glared at him. Finally, the McGregor prompted him to speak.

"You have a message for me?"

"Yes, sir. A verbal message from Sir Niles Conrad of Ravenswood which I was ordered to memorize and deliver." He swallowed and cleared his throat again before continuing. "I will have your ransom in two months' time. I suggest we meet in the middle at the juncture of our respective borders. I hope you have discovered what a conniving liar Alexandra is. It is not important to me that she be returned undefiled; in fact, I am sure she has deserved whatever beatings and despoiling you saw fit to order. Her betrothed, the Sullivan, still wishes to marry her as long as she is well enough to stand for the ceremony." The messenger did not pause to take a breath during his delivery of the speech, and therefore ended up squeaking out the last two words.

Alexandra's stomach clenched in an old familiar fear and revulsion. Her cousin had just given her captors permission to rape and torture her.

The McGregor did not speak for several seconds. He clenched his fists and took a deep breath, before he smiled icily and said, "Tell the Conrad it is with pleasure that I look forward to meeting him."

James nodded for the guards to remove the messenger from the hall. Silence prevailed as the McGregor waited for the messenger to be escorted out. Lifting his wine goblet, he stood and shouted, "To war!" His men repeated the shout and chanted it as they beat their fists noisily upon the wooden tabletops.

Alexandra blinked back tears. Feeling nauseous, she excused herself from the table before she lost composure. Shadowed by her guards, she went straight to her room and lay down. Holding one hand against her stomach, she willed herself not to be sick. She shouldn't have drunk so much wine. Intense hatred for Niles burned within her. For a while, she had actually managed to forget him as she went about the business of learning the ways of the McGregor clan. If this was what one could expect as a prisoner of the Wolf's clan, she'd stay a captive forever rather than set eyes on her cousin again.

From Niles's message, it was obvious he was hopeful she was being treated abominably. She hated the paralyzing fear that rose up in her whenever she thought about him or the abuse she'd suffered at his hands. She feared him more than she hated him, and she wished it was the other way around. At this moment, she craved the courage to kill him herself, and immediately prayed for forgiveness at the thought.

What must the McGregor clan think of her after hearing that message? Did they assume she was some horrible person that deserved to be punished? That her family thought so little of her? She was ashamed and humiliated, and of course, that was exactly how Niles wanted her to feel. Well, she wasn't going to! She'd done nothing her entire life to justify such treatment. She would hold her head high and move amongst the clansmen as she always had.

The only thing she certainly didn't fear was that the McGregor would take action against her upon hearing Niles's message. Ian had honor. He hadn't beaten or raped her, and it wasn't because he was afraid of Niles or the Sullivan's retribution to such treatment. Now, he might try to seduce her, but that was an entirely different matter.

Feeling better and deciding not to pity herself any longer, Alexandra left the chambers to check on young Jamie.

****

Debra's mouth twitched and she struggled to contain her laughter. Her green eyes sparkled with glee as she heard the messenger's recited message. The look of shock and fear that crossed the Englishwoman's face was priceless. Debra decided she'd get along nicely with this Niles of Ravenwood. Perhaps someday she'd be fortunate enough to meet him.

Her thoughts were interrupted by a tug on the hem of her dress. That blasted little beast was at it again. Since no one was paying attention, as they were all busy chanting war cries and pounding on the tables, she took the opportunity to aim a kick at the wolf pup's head. Anticipating the move at the last second, the wolf dodged and took the blow in the shoulder. He yelped and rolled several times before landing on his feet. Baring his teeth, he growled and crouched. Debra's eyes widened when it looked as if the animal was going to attack her, but before he could, a guard scooped him up and took the pest away.

To the boy, she supposed. She'd heard the rumors. He had the run of the castle and was given anything he wanted, including that wolf. When she was his age, she barely had enough to eat and wore tattered clothes. Shuffled from one distant relative to the next when they grew tired of her, and taken in only to be an extra workhand. Yes, what the boy needed was discipline, and with a thick branch across his backside.

****

"I thought you showed great restraint," James said to his brother and slapped him on the back. "For a minute there, I wondered if you were going to strangle the messenger with your bare hands."

"Aye, but I thought it best to save all my anger for the man who deserves it. I'd like to cut out Conrad's tongue and feed it to Happy."

"What kind of trap do you think he's planning?"

"He has to know that Alexandra told me his plans to join in league with the Sullivan to take over our lands, which is why he wants to cast doubt on her truthfulness," Ian said.

"He has to be crazy to think we'll turn over the girl for a ransom, only to have her wed the Sullivan to join forces with him against us," James said.

"Maybe he thinks we'll be tempted by the high ransom amount and that we might not see their combined forces as a threat." Ian bared his teeth wolfishly.

"Chances are, they realize we will be coming to attack them, and they want to control when and where," James added.

"And they obviously aren't planning to hand over any money."

The McGregor brothers sat in silence as they followed their own thoughts. Suddenly, James sat straighter in his chair as if a solution entered his head. With a glint in his eye, he said, "You know, Alexandra has been very good with Jamie. She'd probably make an excellent mother." He glanced over at Ian who remained silent in thought.

James continued, "And she's a very comely lass. Aye, she'd undoubtedly keep a man warm and occupied during the long winter months." Ian glowered at him but remained mute.

Slapping the table as if he'd suddenly solved a problem, James exclaimed, "I know the perfect solution. I'll marry Alexandra! Conrad and Sullivan's plans will be thwarted, and Jamie will finally have a mother!"

Ian lunged across the table at James. Grasping the front of his brother's tunic in one huge fist, he pulled him across the table and drew back his other fist, but before he plowed it into James's face, he saw gleaming laughter in his brother's eyes. Shoving him away, Ian sat back down and covered his face with his hands and released a frustrated sigh.

Laughing, James slapped his brother on the back and said, "Don't worry! It happens to the best of us—although I was beginning to think it would never happen to you. So, when are you going to ask her to marry you?"

Chapter Nine

Alexandra sat in her favorite chair by the hearth and stared into the dying fire. She was not the least tired, and she didn't feel like feigning sleep in order to avoid conversation with the McGregor. In fact, she was anxious to hear his thoughts regarding the message Niles had sent. Her mind drifted to Jamie and Happy. She smiled as she remembered the two of them curled up together in bed when she'd checked. She missed the pup's presence by her side, but seeing the joy the pup brought the boy, she did not have the heart to separate them.

She was still lost in her thoughts when the McGregor entered the room. He appeared surprised to see her still awake, and then he scowled.

"It's been a long day. You should be getting your rest."

"I'm not sleepy."

"Well, I am," the McGregor said. Sitting on the edge of the bed, he removed his boots.

"You must not trust Niles. He would never pay a ransom for me," she warned him.

"Aye, we thought as much. But you needn't worry, for I have decided upon a solution."

She turned away and stared into the fire while he disrobed and settled into the bed.

"We are going to marry," he announced. His voice

sounded strained.

Alexandra whirled around to face him. Her mouth dropped open in shock. She was speechless. Of all the things he could have said, this was the most unexpected. She didn't know what to say or how to react, so she just sat there, stunned. The sound of snoring filled the chamber. How dare he say something like that and then fall asleep! She was tempted to beat on his chest and demand he explain himself, but she was not prepared to hear what he had to say. She needed time to think.

The room grew dark, yet she continued to sit in the chair. Did the McGregor love her? No, certainly not. He acted like he was aggravated with the entire situation. Almost as if he were mad. Then why did he propose? Well, if you could call that a proposal. It was more of an order. She fumed. She wouldn't marry anyone unless she chose to. Did she wish to marry the McGregor? Her stomach did a little flip-flop at the thought. She was definitely attracted to him, but did she love him? Tears came to her eyes. How could she possibly love someone who didn't love her back? And what of her plan to become a nun and serve God? She had been so sure that was what she was meant to do with her life.

She spent a long, restless night tossing upon the pallet. Finally, the sun rose and the darkness receded from the room. She stood up stiffly and looked down at her wrinkled gown. She'd had so much on her mind she hadn't bothered to remove it. Walking over to the side of the bed, she stood and stared down at the McGregor. He lay sleeping peacefully on his back with one arm flung over his head.

"Care to join me?" he asked without opening his

eyes.

Alexandra put her hands on her hips and scowled at him. Ignoring his question, she asked one of her own, "What do you mean we will be married?"

The hand the McGregor had above his head snaked out and grabbed her about the waist. Before she had time to register what was happening, he pulled her into bed and pinned her upper body beneath his.

"I'm tired of lusting after you," he growled, "Do you want me to make love to you now? Or after we are married?"

Her throat tight, she whispered, "After."

The McGregor bent his head, and Alexandra thought he was going to kiss her. Instead, he released her and stood up as she scrambled from the bed.

"Why will we be married?"

He repeated her question. "Why does any man marry? For legitimate heirs, of course."

Babies. Alexandra had not thought about babies. She suddenly had a vision of holding a son in her arms, a son with brown eyes and brown hair like his father. Feeling weak in the knees, she sat back down on the edge of the bed.

"You won't have to worry anymore about Conrad or Sullivan. Our marriage will foil their plans, and as my wife you will be under my protection." He picked his shirt off the floor and slipped it over his head while he talked. "I've sent for the priest, and he will be here in a fortnight."

So soon, she thought, but sat speechless. She needed to think. This was all happening too fast.

Ian dressed while glancing periodically at her face. Did he wonder what she was thinking? Before leaving the room, he told her he would send Maddie to help with any wedding preparations she needed to make.

As soon as the door closed behind him, Alexandra fell back against the bed with one hand covering her stomach. She was still thinking about babies. When she was at the abbey, she never thought she'd get married, let alone have children. As an only child, she had often wished for more brothers and sisters. Now, if she married, she could conceivably have a whole parcel of children. The thought was startling.

Maddie knocked quietly on the chamber door and peeked her head inside. "The laird sent me to assist you?" She appeared puzzled as Alexandra usually took care of her own needs.

It took several seconds before Alexandra could spit out the words. "The McGregor and I are to be married. I would be honored for you to stand with me during the ceremony."

Maddie squealed with delight. She threw herself into Alexandra's arms and gave her a big hug. "I told my mother I thought you and the Wolf were meant to be together!"

Pulling back, Maddie exclaimed, "We've got so much to do. You'll need a fine gown and flowers, and we must decorate the hall. Oh, and Cook needs to be told so she can prepare a special meal."

Overwhelmed, Alexandra pleaded, "Please don't go to too much trouble. I doubt the McGregor wants anything elaborate."

"Don't worry, I'll take care of everything," Maddie said. Obviously eager to spread the news, she fled.

Alexandra stood in the center of the room and wondered what she should do. She felt lost and adrift.

Finally, she decided she might as well check on Jamie and Silas. After changing into a fresh gown, she left the chamber. Her guards for the day waited as usual outside the door. Smiling, she greeted them by name and proceeded to Jamie's bed chamber. The boy's room was empty. Having been ordered to stay in bed yesterday, the lad probably couldn't wait to escape this morning.

She found him in the hall eating his breakfast. Happy sat enthralled at the boy's feet as Jamie slipped him remnants of food. At her approach, the pup yipped and ran toward her. She leaned over and strained to pick him up. He was growing so fast. At this rate he'd be huge when he was full grown. She rubbed her fingers through his fur as the pup licked her chin. Setting him back down on the floor, she laid one hand upon Jamie's head and asked, "And how are you today, my young friend?"

"Good," Jamie replied, his voice muffled with a mouth full of food. He said more, but she couldn't understand what.

"Chew your food first and swallow before answering," she instructed.

Jamie sat and swung his legs back and forth as he did what he was told. The boy seemed to always be in constant motion.

After an exaggerated swallow, he asked, "Can we go see Silas today?"

"After you finish your breakfast, we will be on our way. Your father hasn't restricted you to the keep, has he?"

Smiling, the boy shook his head no, while chewing another large mouthful of food.

They made their way to Silas's hut in the morning sunshine. The temperature was once again warmer than usual, and she wanted to skip right along with young Jamie. Silas had nothing to report. No new illnesses had developed among the clan members during the night. They discussed which herbs were in short supply and how they'd be able to go scouting for them once spring arrived.

Alexandra and Jamie took their time walking back to the keep. She could see the McGregor training his men in the distance. Was he thinking about their wedding? She tried to keep her mind occupied, but thoughts of her upcoming vows crept in, making her anxious. As they entered the great hall, Maddie greeted them.

"Oh good, I don't have to search all over for you. I've found several dresses for you to try, and I'm preparing a hot bath." She pulled on Alexandra's hand to hurry her along. Young Jamie opted to go back outside.

"Where did you get the dresses?" Alexandra asked as they walked up to the bed chamber.

Maddie hesitated and then said, "They belonged to James's wife. She was an Englishwoman too. She had many dresses. These are a few that were left behind."

"What happened to her? I've never heard anyone speak of her."

Sorrow entered Maddie's eyes and she said, "It's best to ask James or the Wolf."

Alexandra made a mental note to do just that. She approached the bed and looked at the three dresses draped over it. One immediately caught her eye. It was a sky-blue velvet. Picking up the sleeve, she rubbed it between her fingertips. It was so soft.

"I don't believe she ever wore that one. It's not hemmed, and there are no buttons on the back," she said. "Let's see how it fits."

Maddie helped her out of her clothes and assisted in pulling the velvet dress over her head.

"It feels wonderful," Alexandra said, as she ran her hands over the garment.

"As does it look," Maddie returned and circled around her. "The waist needs to be taken in a little, but that will be easy enough. A couple more inches need to go from the bottom before we hem it. We just need buttons. I will have plenty of time to finish."

"I can help you," Alexandra offered, although sewing wasn't something she enjoyed.

"Oh no, miss. My younger sisters will be happy to assist."

****

Word of the upcoming nuptials traveled surprisingly fast among the clan. Over the next few days, Alexandra received many congratulations, as well as curious looks and a few hostile glares. After saving young Jamie, she noticed the clan's attitude toward her had softened. She was kept busy trying to remember everyone's name, and who was related to whom.

Her days were routine. She slept by the hearth, and the McGregor didn't protest. He was up and gone before she even awoke. He seemed to avoid being alone with her. After she broke her fast, she'd check on young Jamie and his constant companion Happy. The two were now inseparable, and it was a joy to watch them play together. With her small companions in tow, she would head for Silas's hut to see what the day had in store. Silas was a gruff, but excellent teacher, and Alexandra was learning much.

Today, he told her, they were off to set a child's broken arm.

The girl, Fiona, was ten years of age. Her mother hovered as they examined her arm. Alexandra thought it looked broken in two places below the elbow, and Silas agreed. The setting was going to be very painful. Alexandra asked the mother to make tea, and she gave her some medicinal herbs to add to it. The brew would help to calm the girl and make her sleepy. While Fiona drank her tea, Alexandra asked her how she'd hurt herself.

"I was climbing trees with my friends. We were racing to see who could climb the highest. I was winning," she said and then frowned. "But the branches were slippery, and I fell."

Remembering all too well her own recent experience, Alexandra said, "I am so sorry you got hurt doing something you love. When I was your age, I also loved to climb trees. Perhaps when your arm is healed, we can climb some together. When the branches are no longer slippery, of course. Would you like that?"

Both mother and daughter smiled, looking amused at the thought of the laird's soon-to-be wife climbing trees. "And look," Alexandra said and held up her braid, "we have the same color hair." She leaned closer to look in the child's eyes, and exclaimed, "We have the same color eyes too! I think we are destined to be friends, don't you?"

Fiona nodded emphatically.

"You must be very sure to follow Silas's orders so your arm will heal properly. This is going to hurt very much, but I know what a brave girl you are."

As Alexandra encouraged Fiona, Silas gathered what he needed.

"Give her this to bite down on," he said, and handed over a small, thick piece of leather. "I will elongate the arm and hold it in place while you put the sticks on each side and wrap it." Speaking to the mother, he said, "Place your hands on her shoulders and keep her still." He looked at both women and asked, "Any questions?"

Alexandra shook her head and held the piece of leather up to the girl's mouth. She bit down on it. Alexandra put on a brave face and nodded assuredly at Fiona.

The setting went well. Silas pulled Fiona's arm straight. and the girl screamed but did not move. Alexandra quickly wrapped the strips of cloth and tied them off. Silas placed her arm gently down onto the bed. Both mother and child stifled tears.

"You are truly the bravest girl I know," Alexandra said and squeezed the child's good hand.

After giving the mother extra instructions and reassuring her they'd be back to check on Fiona, they left and headed back toward the keep.

Alexandra did not speak as they walked. She was deep in thought. Giving out herbs and medicinal brews was the easy part of healing. Dealing with the screams and the pain was an entirely different matter and it troubled her.

Silas interrupted her by muttering, "We make a good team."

"Aye, we do," she smiled. They seemed to be able to read each other's minds and worked well together without much discussion.

"Thank you," she said. "That's the best compliment you could give me."

He grunted and picked up his pace to get ahead of her. "Well, don't let it go to your head, you still have an awful lot to learn," he said back over his shoulder as he headed toward his hut.

Alexandra automatically slowed her pace as she passed the training field. Her eyes searched for and found the McGregor. Just the sight of the man and the sound of his voice stirred her heart. He was observing and yelling out commands to two young men who were circling each other and fighting without weapons. Alexandra watched as she strolled by. When the McGregor was no longer in sight, she picked up her pace. She looked forward to dining with him this evening. Entering the keep, she found her time to be on her own as young Jamie and Happy were nowhere around. She prayed they were keeping out of mischief.

Maddie was only too happy to comply with Alexandra's wish for another bath. The girl was always so cheerful and pleasant, eager to accommodate any wish. As servants brought up buckets of steaming water, Maddie chattered on about the wedding plans. The whole event didn't seem real to Alexandra. She just wanted to relax in the tub and she told Maddie she would be able to take care of herself. Maddie seemed relieved to be getting back to her 'wedding duties' and with another, "I'm so excited!" she bounced out of the chamber.

Moments later as she was preparing to step into the tub, she heard a soft knock. Wrapping a blanket around herself, she cracked the door open but no one was there.

She moved to shut it and spotted a tray with tea and shortbread on the floor. Maddie was so thoughtful.

The water was wonderfully warm and silky against her skin. Alexandra slid down farther into the tub and rested her head back against the rim. Closing her eyes, she relaxed and let the tension drift out of her body. Her thoughts turned to, who else, but the McGregor. Was she being a fool for not running again? It would be easy to slip away, but with no knowledge of the area she'd probably get lost and starve to death, if she didn't die from exposure first. Where could she go anyway? She couldn't go back to the abbey. That was the first place Niles would look, and she had no means of supporting herself.

Staying with the McGregor was the right choice. It was really the only option, but did that mean she'd failed God and her life's mission? Surely, if there was another way out, God would show her. Her feelings of failure conflicted with her growing attraction for Ian. Was she going to be badly hurt?

Restless at the direction her thoughts were taking, she sat upright in the tub and took a sip of the tea from the tray she'd put next to the tub. Grimacing from its bitter taste, she set the cup aside and picked up the shortbread. Much better, she thought as she nibbled on it. Well, she'd best get accustomed to the idea of getting married, because the date was quickly approaching.

She stood in the tub and let the water cascade down her body before reaching for her drying cloth. The room swayed, and she started to sway with it. Clutching the side of the tub like an anchor, she waited for the wave of dizziness to pass. It passed but was replaced by a rolling nausea. Alexandra attempted to get out of the tub as quickly as she could, but before she could lift her other leg out, another wave of dizziness slammed into her. She felt herself falling backward and flailed her arms to regain her balance or to find something sturdy to grab onto. Her fingertips snagged her drying cloth before she toppled to the floor. She tucked in her head, and her shoulders took the brunt of the fall. The leg that had been in the tub landed sorely on its rim.

What was wrong with her? She managed to pull the drying cloth over her naked body before curling into a ball as the next wave of nausea hit. She heard pounding on the chamber door and her name called. She tried to answer, but her voice lacked strength.

She heard several voices out in the hallway before the door opened and Maddie rushed in. She could see the feet of others standing beyond the doorway.

"What happened? We heard a loud noise," Maddie exclaimed and knelt down beside her.

Alexandra, unable to lift her head, looked up into Maddie's worried eyes and pleaded, "McGregor," before she turned aside and retched.

Chapter Ten

Alexandra didn't know how long she lay on the floor, alternating between cycles of dizziness and vomiting. Sweet Maddie stayed with her, holding her hand and wiping her face clean.

She knew when the McGregor entered the room by the sound and vibrations of the floor boards. He lifted her up into his arms, like a baby. The movement brought on intense dizziness, and she clutched the front of his shirt. With sweat now running off her face, she looked up into the McGregor's dark, intense eyes. She tried to get the words out, but it was a struggle. He leaned and turned his ear closer to her mouth, and she whispered, "Poison?" before she went limp in his arms.

He gently laid her upon the bed before he turned his attention to the servants who crowded the door.

"Summon Silas," he roared, "Now!" Several servants scurried from the doorway. Glancing about the room, he asked Maddie, who sat anxiously at Alexandra's side, "What has she eaten today besides what's on that tray?"

"I brought her porridge this morning, but that is all. I did not order or bring up the tray."

He strode to the doorway. "Did anyone bring this tray up? Did you see who did?" he questioned all those huddled in the hall.

The servants looked at each other and murmured

amongst themselves. They compared where they'd been and what they'd been doing, before answering or shaking their heads no. Ian ushered everyone out of the room issuing one last order as he shut the door, "Find my brother."

****

Silas's report was not good. He agreed it looked like Alexandra had indeed been poisoned. He walked over to the tray and picked up a biscuit, sniffing it before setting it back down. He stuck his finger in the tea and brought it up to his nose before touching the finger to the tip of his tongue. "Probably the tea," he said, and walked back to stand next to the McGregor at Alexandra's bedside. Silas shook his head as he looked down at her unconscious body.

"There's naught I can do," he said, lifting his empty hands into the air. "She will either live or die, depending on how much poison she consumed and how strong her will is to survive." Before he left the chamber, Silas laid a hand on McGregor's shoulder and said gruffly, "Only time will tell. Keep her warm and dry."

Alone with Alexandra, Ian sat on the bed next to her and stared at her beautiful, pale face. She was breathing slow and shallow. Flickering flames of anger rose as a fire blazed within. *Who would dare to do such a thing?* If she died, he would find and choke the life out of this person, or persons, with his bare hands.

He took her tiny hand between his, marveling at how small it looked in his. He leaned his face closer to hers. "Woman, don't be thinking this is your way out. You are to be mine. I'd like to see some of the spunk you displayed when you found out I was the Wolf.

Come back to me. We have much fighting, and aye, much love-making to do."

****

Debra cradled her laundry basket on her swaying hip and exited the keep. She headed toward her hut. Her heart was still beating fast. She'd gotten away with it! She smirked as she considered how clever she'd been.

Like the other women, she brought her laundry to the keep to scrub by the warmth of the huge fireplace in the main hall. The womenfolk gathered here to wash and gossip. They were allowed freedom to enter the kitchen to help themselves to drink and daily pastries. Debra had carried the vial of poison in her pocket every day, waiting for an opportunity to use it.

She'd witnessed the servants carrying water up to the laird's bedchamber, and she had seized the moment. Excitement was in the air today as plans for the upcoming wedding were discussed. In the kitchen, Cook and her staff had gathered to plan menu options for the big meal. Women came in and out all day, so it was not a surprise when the kitchen staff didn't bother to look up as she'd made herself a tea tray. Turning her back on them, she'd kept the tray low in front of her as she exited.

When she got to her basket of clothes, she'd laid the tray on top and covered it with a wet garment. Walking through the main hall and up the main staircase, she'd glanced around, but no one was paying any attention to her. Reaching the top of the stair, she'd gazed at the room below. The coast was clear. She'd hurried to the bedchamber door which was just out of sight of the stairs. Her hands shaking, she'd removed the small tray from her basket and had set it before the door. While listening for footsteps or voices, she'd taken the poison from her pocket and held it briefly over the cup. How much to give? She would have liked to keep some for future use, but wanting to make sure the bitch would die, she'd poured the entire contents into the cup and had given it a quick stir with her finger. She'd knocked softly on the door, but as she'd picked up her basket, she'd heard a creak from the steps. She couldn't go down that way or she'd be seen. Instead, she'd run silently around the corner and through the back hall, escaping down an empty servant's stairway.

Debra chuckled to herself as she thought of the English beauty writhing in pain. She was so deep in thought she almost missed the laird's brother walking toward her in the distance. *This was definitely her day!* She'd practiced several different scenarios in her head just in case of a chance meeting. The path before her was fairly clear with the exception of intermittent puddles that had iced over. Her timing needed to be perfect. As he drew close enough for her to nod and smile at, Debra stepped onto an icy patch and shifted her weight ever so slightly. She went down in an instant. Her teeth jarred together and she cried out in real pain. One foot lay straight in front, while the other was twisted beneath her bottom. She moaned in both real and feigned pain. Grabbing her ankle, she willed tears to her eyes. James ran over and squatted beside her. "That was quite a fall you took. Are you okay?"

She looked up at him with tearful eyes. "I think I may have wrenched my ankle," she said and tried to stand.

James clasped his hands under her elbows and

pulled her upright. Debra took a hesitant step and pretended her ankle gave out. She would have fallen if he hadn't held on.

"It's obvious you're not going to be able to walk. Can you stand on one foot while I pick up your clothes?" he asked, holding her steady.

"Yes, thank you."

James kept an eye on her, probably to make sure she didn't topple over as he picked up her scattered clothes and put them back in her basket. He handed her the basket and swooped her up in his arms. "I'll take you back to the keep and we'll see if Silas or Alexandra is around to take a look at that ankle."

Debra leaned her head against his shoulder. "You're so kind. I can't thank you enough," she said huskily, looking up at him through her eyelashes.

She held tightly to the basket with her right hand and reached her left arm up and around his neck. The result of that move bought her left breast in direct contact with his chest. She held on tightly as if she were afraid he was going to drop her and pressed herself closer yet. James glanced down at her, and she smiled coyly up at him, hoping he wasn't too stupid to understand what she was offering.

She saw interest flare in his eyes. He pulled her tighter against his chest and smiled knowingly at her unspoken offer.

"Is there someone I can inform of your injury? I'm sorry but I can't seem to recall your name. Are you Doreen?"

Debra smiled through gritted teeth. The fool should know her name by now. "It's Debra."

"Robert's woman?" he questioned.

She saw he already knew the answer when the lustful look in his eyes was replaced with disdain.

"My lord!" a clan guard yelled out as he ran up to intercept them. "Your brother needs you immediately. He's in his chamber." James turned and unceremoniously dumped her into the surprised guard's arms. Debra watched as he ran toward the keep without a word or backward glance.

****

Alexandra woke to the painful glare of the sun's morning rays. She groaned and covered her eyes. Her mouth was so dry she could barely swallow. Was she sick? Disoriented, she propped herself up on one elbow and squinted against the sun's daggers. The McGregor was in bed with her. She leaned over and frowned down on him. "Why am I in your bed?"

The McGregor laughed freely and wrapped his arms around her. Pulling her close, he lifted a brow in a way she found provocative and whispered, "You mean you don't remember?"

Alexandra couldn't remember a thing, but she had a wallop of a headache, and her body ached like it had been trampled by wild horses. Did she drink too much wine? Had she been indecent?

The McGregor chuckled. "Put your mind at rest, woman. Your innocence remains unscathed."

He released her and slipped out of bed. He opened the door and told one of the guardsmen to summon Silas and Maddie.

Alexandra stood and leaned against the bed to steady herself.

Ian turned around. "Get back in bed," he ordered, all playfulness gone from his voice. "You were poisoned. Three days ago to be exact."

"What?" She sat back on the bed. She stretched her memory, trying to think of the last thing she could recall. Scenes from setting the girl's arm, to watching the McGregor on the field, to watching servants fill the copper tub, flashed in rapid succession until she remembered rising from the tub. She felt queasy at the thought. Her hand instinctively went to her stomach. "I remember," she said.

The McGregor came over and assisted her to climb back into bed. "You will stay there until Silas has a chance to check you over and gives you permission to get up."

Maddie knocked on the door. The McGregor left as she entered. "I was so worried," Maddie said and tears filled her eyes. She put down the bedding she carried to give Alexandra a gentle hug.

"I can't believe I've been asleep for three days. What's been going on?" *And who would want me dead?*

"The McGregor rarely left your side. Only when I came in to attend you did he leave." Maddie laid out a fresh nightgown and put a clean washcloth in the basin of water she'd set at Alexandra's bedside. "There's been much talk about who did this to you, but no one seems to have witnessed anything." She squeezed excess water from the washcloth and handed it to Alexandra. "Silas will be here soon. Let's get you freshened up."

Silas checked her over and proclaimed she needed to stay in bed for at least another day, during which time she was to drink plentifully to cleanse the poison from her system. His only display of emotion was to pat her hand before he left, and to tell her in that gruff tone of his that he expected to see her bright and early outside his hut the next morn.

Maddie brought in a pitcher of fresh water and informed her that the McGregor had left orders for Alexandra to only drink or eat from food presented by herself or the laird. Alexandra sat up in bed and took the mug she was offered. She was profoundly thirsty, and she emptied the pitcher in no time. At this rate, she'd be on the chamber pot all day.

When Maddie brought up a second pitcher, she said with a smile, "You have friends who have been beside themselves at not being able to see you. Shall I let them in?"

Alexandra heard whining and pleading outside the door. She smiled at the increasing pitch and said, "Please do."

The moment the door was cracked open, a flying ball of fur flew toward her, followed by a little boy yelling, "Wait! I said wait for me!" The pup turned a deaf ear. Without slowing his stride, he launched himself into the air, just managing to get his front paws onto the top edge of the bed, and using his strength, he pulled himself all the way up.

Happy was in her face, licking it no matter which way she turned. Her laughter only excited him more, and he doubled his efforts, his butt wagging in fast time with his tail. Young Jamie jumped up on the bed and pulled Happy away, holding the struggling pup to his side. "Sorry," he said, hanging his head.

"No, no. You two are my best medicine," she replied, catching her breath.

Alexandra's young friends kept her entertained throughout the day. Jamie told her stories and showed her toys he'd made. He demonstrated new tricks he'd taught Happy. "Father says he's going to grow really big, so if I want to keep him he has to learn to listen to me."

Alexandra agreed to help him with the project and said, "We'll work with him every day."

By late afternoon she was extremely tired, barely able to keep her eyes open. She sent them on a mission to find and bring back pretty stones and bird feathers.

****

When the McGregor entered his bed chambers before evening meal, he found all three asleep in his bed. Alexandra lay peacefully under the furs with a hand resting on Jamie's stomach. Young Jamie was sprawled atop the furs on one side of Alexandra, while the wolf pup lay curled behind her bent knees on the other side. The pup opened his eyes and acknowledged Ian's presence, but otherwise remained comfortably still.

Ian was envious. He'd like to be curled up next to her too. He watched her a few moments before he decided she needed her rest more than he needed her company. Shaking his head, he slipped quietly from the room. He had it bad, whatever "it" was. He chided himself. How the sight of a sick woman, in bed with a boy and a dog, could make him lust for her, was beyond him. He'd never burned this badly for a woman. As far as he was concerned, his wedding night could not come soon enough.

Chapter Eleven

To everyone's amazement, Alexandra was up, dressed and ready to go about her business at the crack of dawn. She hoped to be early enough to surprise Silas and catch him still asleep. Chuckling at the thought, she exited the chamber and found two men guarding the door.

"Oh no, not again." She sighed. "Please tell me you're not going to follow me around all day?"

Finn and McAlistair nodded in unison. McAlistair bowed and gestured her forward with his hand. "After you, m'lady."

Might as well make the best of it she thought and led the way, at least until she had a few words with the McGregor.

She pounded on Silas's door and did indeed wake him up. She refrained from smiling as he puttered about, muttering under his breath. They checked on the child, Fiona, and changed the wrap covering her arm. The girl was quick to remind Alexandra of her promise to go tree climbing. "I am looking forward to it," she replied.

The rest of the day was spent at Silas's table pouring over his drawings of medicinal herbs. He was a good artist, and she easily recognized his renditions. On the margins of the scrolled paper, he'd made notes as to usages and doses. Alexandra was impressed by the amount of time he must have spent working on the project. She came to the conclusion he was doing this for the benefit of his clan, should he pass on. Most of the herbs she was familiar with, but there were still many she had no knowledge of. Silas also showed her where he stored his supplies, pointing out the many near empty baskets he was eager to fill when the weather stayed warmer.

It was well into the afternoon when young Jamie showed up with Happy in tow. The guardsmen managed to keep them busy for a while, but it wasn't long before the boy started pleading with forlorn brown eyes, for her to play. After throwing sticks for the pup and running races, Alexandra decided it was time to think of new games. The lad was smart; perhaps she could teach him the rudiments of chess. She knew Jamie preferred the freedom of being outside, but after he'd run off his excess energy, the game might be a good way to settle him down at night.

The main hall was fairly empty when they arrived back at the keep. A few women remained finishing up their wash, and the kitchen staff was busy preparing for the dinner hour. She and Jamie picked out a spot across from the center fireplace, and she set up one of the chess sets made available to all. Today's lesson was easy. She showed him the pieces, their names, and how they were allowed to move across the board. It brought back loving memories of when her father taught her to play. Jamie proved an avid learner and before long, he recited the information back to her. He was eager to start a game, but as dinner would soon be ready, she told him it would give them both something to look forward to before tomorrow's evening meal.

Maddie and Cook approached as she put the game away. "Cook would like to go over the menu for the special day," Maddie said.

Alexandra turned and smiled apologetically at the portly cook. "I'm sorry. I can't seem to remember your name."

Cook gave a hearty laugh, "That's because it's been Cook for longer than I can remember. I don't think I'd answer to anything else."

They went over the menu together, and Alexandra told her it looked fabulous, and she thanked Cook in advance for all her hard work. The two women left her and headed back toward the kitchen. She had sent Jamie up to his room to get cleaned up for evening meal, so she sat alone with her thoughts before she too needed to change.

The wedding day was fast approaching. She managed to block it from her mind most of the time, unless someone brought the subject up, and then she'd feel her stomach drop. She wasn't sure whether it was due to fear or anticipation or a combination of both. Was she jumping out of the frying pan and into the fire? Since her poisoning, she hadn't seen much of Ian, except at evening meals.

"Excuse me, but I was told you might be able to help me?"

Alexandra looked up to find the red-haired, large-bosomed woman standing beside her. She remembered her from the first evening at the keep as the lady with the hateful stares.

"I'm sorry. I don't think we've been introduced."

Holding out her hand, the woman said, "My name is Debra. Debra McCaw. I am Robert's woman."

With reservation, Alexandra shook Debra's hand, and asked, "How can I assist you?"

The woman dropped down in the vacant chair next to her and started unlacing her boot. As she did so, she told of having taken a bad fall on the ice a few weeks back, and of how her ankle didn't seem to be healing.

Alexandra lifted the injured foot and set it on her lap. Fading black and blue bruises lined the inner side. She gently palpated for broken bones but found none. Placing the foot back on the ground, she said, "I don't think there's a break, but there is still some swelling. You should stay off it and elevate it as much as you can. It will take some time to heal."

"Thank you so much for taking a look," Debra said. "I am sorry if I did not make you welcome when you first arrived." Resting her hands on her knees and looking down at her feet, she said, "I have very bad memories of the English, but I know I am wrong to blame you personally."

Alexandra was warmed by the woman's apology. She briefly touched the woman's hand and said, "Let's put the past behind us. We can move forward and get to know each other for who we really are."

****

Alexandra woke from a nightmare. Startled, she rose to a sitting position. Tears coursed down her face and she choked back a sob. Visions of the horrible dream played in her head. The McGregor was held captive again, chained to the floor. But this time, her cousin Niles sliced and jabbed at him with a sword. The Sullivan held her tightly, laughing at her struggles to push him away, and prevented her from going to Ian's aid. She woke just as Niles raised his sword over his head with both hands, ready to plunge it into the McGregor's heart.

Taking deep breaths, Alexandra lay back down and tried to calm herself. The nightmare brought back all the fear and ugliness of her past. Bile rose in her throat. She swallowed it back and pushed herself from the floor to splash cold water on her face from the basin. The nausea subsided and the memories faded like tendrils of smoke, but their stench remained.

Tomorrow, she was to be married. Time had passed too quickly, and she didn't feel any better prepared. Now new questions entered her thoughts. Was she putting the McGregor at risk by marrying him? Surely not? Since they would be married, there was no need for him to pick up a ransom from Niles. Soon she would be the property of the McGregor, and Niles could do nothing about it. Even if the unthinkable happened, and Niles somehow managed to kill Ian, she would then belong to her husband's family, so Niles had nothing to gain by those actions, except of course, to torment her.

Calming herself with reassurances, she dressed quickly, anxious to get on with her day so she could think about something or someone other than herself. She found Jamie and Silas waiting and wondering about her whereabouts. She brushed off their questions and asked who they were off to see first. Leading the way along the snow-melted, muddy path, Alexandra turned her attentions to Jamie, and asked him to recall the names of the chess pieces.

No major illnesses needed tending that afternoon. Silas supervised as Alexandra stitched up the palm of a warrior's hand. His training opponent had been young and a little too eager. They also distributed a cough tonic and medicinal rub to several families. By the time their day was finished, her skirts and her boots were caked in mud, making it difficult to walk. Both Jamie and Happy were filthy from head to toe and seemed pleased about it. When the trio arrived back at the keep, Alexandra walked them around to the back servants' entrance off the kitchen, where she turned Jamie and the pup over to his dismayed nursemaid.

****

The eve of the wedding, Maddie had Alexandra's dinner sent up to the room. She missed the laughing companionship of the McGregor and his clan while she ate alone. She had not seen him on the practice field that day either. She didn't have much of an appetite, and she pushed the food around the plate. Maddie knocked on the door and entered.

"The McGregor said to inform you he will not be joining you in the bed chamber tonight. He will see you at the ceremony tomorrow."

Alexandra was both relieved and disappointed at the same time. "Did he say what he was doing?"

"I think he plans on spending the evening with his brother."

Maddie left with the food tray, and Alexandra restlessly paced around the room. She was nervous, and she doubted whether she'd be able to sleep at all. Tomorrow, she'd be a married woman. Married to the Wolf. *Dear God, please tell me I'm doing the right thing, that this is Your will.* No doubt being married to, and having the protection of the McGregor, was a much better alternative than being in her cousin's monstrous hands. Perhaps this was God's answer to her prayer for escape, but would Ian ever love her?

After several hours of pacing, the big bed started to look inviting. She crawled in under the furs and sank into the softness. The fire she had just stoked burned brightly, and she lay back and watched the shadows dance upon the walls. She fell asleep in the midst of praying.

****

The time had arrived. Alexandra, dressed in the blue velvet dress, sat in the chair facing the fire while Maddie removed remnants of rolled, tied cloth from her hair. Running a comb through the individual curls, Maddie exclaimed, "Your hair has turned out even better than I expected. The Wolf will not be able to take his eyes off you."

At the mention of the McGregor's nickname, the butterflies in Alexandra's stomach fluttered. She was both anxious and nervous to see the McGregor. Was he having any second thoughts?

Maddie worked with Alexandra's hair, adding dried flowers and ribbons as she saw fit. Finally, she stepped back and said, "Perfect." Maddie herself was dressed in a blue woolen dress, and Alexandra thought her untamed red curls looked lovely against the dark blue.

"I'll see if they're ready for us yet," Maddie said and slipped out the bedroom door.

As Alexandra waited for her to return, she heard the rumbling of many voices coming from below. How many people were here? Maddie reappeared several minutes later.

"It's time!" she said excitedly, her face flushed.

Alexandra walked to the door and paused. Taking a

deep breath, she slowly let it out and then nodded. Maddie handed her an arrangement of dried flowers and opened the door to lead the way. Surprisingly, she still had two guards outside the door. They smiled as she walked by. Would she continue to be guarded after she was married?

Alexandra and Maddie paused when they reached the top of the stairs. Looking down, she saw the hall packed with familiar faces. The entire clan, including the children, appeared to be present. As the two women approached, silence, like a wave, washed over the crowd, and they divided leaving a pathway open to the McGregor, who stood waiting in front of the priest.

****

Ian, with his brother by his side, turned to face the steps. He stared, stunned at the beautiful vision who walked toward him. Alexandra looked like an angel. Her long hair flowed and curled around her, and she wore a form-fitting dress that clung to her womanly curves and matched the color of her eyes. Feeling his brother's hard elbow poke him in the ribs, Ian shut his open mouth but continued to stare. He offered his hand as Alexandra drew close, and clasped her hand in his, but she did not meet his eyes. He turned with her and faced the priest. The clergyman droned on for several minutes about something, but Ian wasn't paying much attention. His focus was on the woman standing next to him. He could feel her small hand trembling within his like a bird trying to escape. The priest suddenly stopped speaking and looked expectantly at him.

"I do," he replied.

The priest spoke more and then paused, and looked in Alexandra's direction, waiting for her reply.

She stood frozen. The McGregor gave her hand a squeeze and caressed her knuckles with his thumb. She took a gasping breath and said, "I do."

Alexandra's eyes widened when Ian pulled a gold medallion ring from his pocket. It was far too large to ever fit her hand, but he had it on a delicate, gold chain. Lifting her hand, he placed the ring in her palm and closed her fingers around it. As the priest pronounced them husband and wife, a roaring cheer erupted from the clan, followed by shouts of "Kiss your wife!" Ian placed both hands around Alexandra's waist and hoisted her up in the air as if she weighed nothing. With her feet off the ground, she grabbed his upper arms in surprise, and he brought his lips to hers in a lingering kiss. The crowd roared and cheered once more.

Alexandra's face was flushed when he released her. The clan members then immediately surrounded them and offered handshakes, slaps on the back, and hugs of congratulations.

****

Debra sat stiff and unmoving during the ceremony with a smile plastered on her face. Bitter gall rose up in her throat, and she swallowed repeatedly. She wanted to scream. She wanted to hit and punch and rip someone's hair out. Preferably blonde hair. Her breathing quickened as did the rise and fall of her chest. Tears of frustration trespassed into her eyes. Nooo! Finally, the ceremony concluded. People rose to their feet, cheering.

"Happy tears. Happy tears," she said to Robert and to the couple standing next to them and dabbed her eyes with her kerchief.

****

The celebrations started immediately with pints of

ale and tables laden with food. Cook must have started baking the minute she received the news. Ian escorted Alexandra to their usual table where James and Jamie joined them.

"Father says I can call you Aunt Alexandra now." The boy grinned from ear to ear. "And you don't ever have to leave. We can play every day! Forever!"

Alexandra smiled at the boy's enthusiasm. "If I'm your aunt, then you must be my nephew. I've never had a nephew before."

Ian filled her glass with wine and put food on their plates. She realized she was still clutching his ring. She'd been holding it so tight indentions were left in her hand. The ring was beautiful. The gold shimmered in the candlelight. Etchings of a full-bodied wolf were on one side and a wolf's head was on the other. As she turned it she noted an inscription inside. She read both of their names and the date. Her eyes filled with tears at his unexpected thoughtfulness. She glanced over at him, but he was in conversation with James. She slipped the delicate chain over her head and lifted her hair free.

Alexandra looked at the mound of food he'd piled on her plate and knew that she wouldn't be able to do it justice. She patted her leg under the table and Happy responded by leaving Jamie's side to come sit at her feet. While everyone was talking and laughing, she snuck large morsels of food to the pup. Pushing her food around on the plate, she tried to taste everything since Cook had gone to so much trouble.

Ian leaned over and whispered in her ear, "You keep that up, and he's going to get fat."

She hadn't realized anyone had noticed. "I don't

want to hurt Cook's feelings. I guess I'm just not very hungry."

Ian leaned over again and brushed her hair back from her neck. "And what, I wonder, is on your mind?" he whispered, and placed a gentle kiss on her neck, just below her ear.

Alexandra blushed and looked to see if anyone was paying attention. Many smiling faces turned her way.

"Come to think of it, I'm not very hungry either," Ian said and pushed himself up from the table. Grabbing her hand, he pulled her up from her seat and led her from the hall. As people noticed, shouts and teasing comments followed them. Within seconds, the entire hall cheered once more.

Alexandra was shocked and speechless. Surely he wasn't taking her to bed in the middle of the afternoon? Ian led her up the steps and to the bedchamber. She paused in front of the door, and Ian gave her a gentle push into the room.

She wasn't mentally prepared for this; she thought she'd have until late that evening. Clearing her throat, she said, "Shouldn't we be entertaining our guests?"

"They can entertain themselves." Ian advanced toward her and as he did, she backed away until she felt the bed behind her knees. Ian continued to walk toward her until she put her arms straight out with both palms planted against the middle of his chest to hold him away. Ian pulled her hands from his chest and brought them up to his lips. Staring seriously down into her blue eyes, he whispered, "Have I ever given you cause to fear me?"

"No," she replied and reminded herself how honorable he was. She relaxed a little as her instinct told her she could trust him.

Ian gently pulled her into his arms. Hugging her, he ran his hands over her back and hips while he nuzzled her neck. Goose bumps broke out over her skin as he sucked and kissed the line from her neck to her jaw. She wrapped her arms around him and he brought her closer, his lips covering hers. Cupping her buttocks, he drew her up against him. Their tongues met and danced before his plunged deeper into her mouth. He made her feel so good, so alive. She wanted to get closer to him. She needed to get closer to him. He undid the back of her dress, and his warm hands caressed her bare skin.

Alexandra had the sudden desire to feel his skin beneath her hands. She lifted the hem of his shirt and stood on tiptoe. Ian raised his arms and helped her remove it. He stood silent and unmoving as she explored his body. She ran her hands over his muscular chest and arms. Under her fingertips, his skin was soft and smooth, belying the hidden strength beneath in the rippling muscles. She inhaled his clean woodsy scent and leaned in to press her lips against the jagged scar on his arm. Ian yanked her flush against him with one arm and lifted her chin with the other hand. He bent and engulfed her mouth in a deep, slow kiss which she hungrily returned. She felt his hands on her shoulders, and he slowly lowered the top of her gown to her waist and held her sleeves as she pulled her arms from the garment. He then slid the gown over her hips and let it fall to the floor. He held out his hands to her. She clasped them and stepped out of the dress. Ian stared at her and heat rose up over her cheeks. She fought the urge to cover herself, knowing the thin cotton shift did little to hide her nudity. Ian gathered her close once more and kissed her tenderly, teasing her lips with his tongue and then more fully until she was breathless and aching for more. He stopped kissing her only long enough to pull the shift over her head.

"You are so beautiful," he whispered and pulled her naked body back against his. His hands seemed to be everywhere at once. Down her back, to her buttocks and thighs, before he cupped a breast and rubbed his thumb across her nipple. Alexandra gasped and moaned as a jolt of pleasure went straight to her womb.

Not wanting to be the only one completely naked, she tugged downward on his pants. His hands left her body to untie the drawstring. She took a step backward when she saw his large, throbbing manhood.

She stuttered. "I-I-don't see how this can possibly work."

Ian laughed. "Believe me; you are going to be surprised at just *how good* this is going to work."

Alexandra remained doubtful but let Ian lift her onto the bed. Joining her, he tugged her slightly stiff body back into his arms and caressed her. He said, "I will take things as slowly as you need me to. The first time can be painful for a woman, but I'm told the pain is fleeting."

Their legs entwined, and the hard ridge of his manhood pressed against her stomach.

He kissed her and moved his hands up and down her body. She relaxed again and simply enjoyed the sensations he aroused. Ian rolled her onto her back and rained kisses down her neck and collarbone before he cupped a breast. Lowering his head, he flicked the nipple with his tongue until it puckered and she arched off the bed. He took the nipple into his mouth and gently sucked and tugged on it. She felt she was melting and yet filled with a yearning she didn't understand.

Ian turned his attention to her other breast and moved one hand caressingly down over her stomach and then lower. He stroked the insides of her thighs with his fingertips before settling his hand over her mound and finding the small nub of her womanhood. He gently feathered his thumb across it, and she bucked in surprise at the intimacy of his touch. *Dear God, what was he doing to her?*

She breathed heavier. She needed more. This was an exquisite type of torture. Ian settled himself between her thighs and positioned himself. He leaned down and kissed her intimately, and thrust deep into her. A sudden stab of pain elevated her out of the fog of desire. She groaned into his mouth and tensed.

"Shhh. Just let it pass," he whispered. Holding himself still, he brushed the hair back from her face and kissed her hairline. He tenderly kissed her until the tension left her body. He began to slowly move inside her.

The sensation was not totally unpleasant. Her body was stretched to the maximum, but the pain was nearly gone. He nuzzled her neck, and the movement inside her quickened, until he suddenly stopped moving and stiffened. With a guttural sound of release, he collapsed on top of her. After several moments, she couldn't breathe and she attempted to push him off. Ian rolled over onto his back and pulled her with him, tucking her head onto his shoulder. Neither spoke, and it wasn't long before she heard him snoring.

Alexandra lay awake thinking about what had just

happened. So was that the marital duty she'd heard some women talk about as being so distasteful? It wasn't that bad. In fact, a few parts of it were rather nice. She supposed she'd be able to fulfill her wifely duties whenever the McGregor desired them.

****

Alexandra's body glistened with sweat and she panted faster and faster. Her head was tilted back and her hair lay splayed out against the pillow. She clutched Ian's biceps as her pleasure grew and intensified. She was climbing higher and higher toward some unattainable goal just out of her grasp, until finally, an explosion of satisfaction washed over her bringing waves of immense pleasure and release until she floated back to earth.

Ian rolled onto his back pulling Alexandra with him until she lay completely on top of him, her legs between his, and her head resting on the center of his chest. Still breathless, she lifted her head and met his brown eyes. "That...was absolutely amazing," she whispered.

Ian grinned, obviously very pleased with her reaction. He gave her bottom a quick smack, and boasted, "Of course it was. I am good at everything I do."

She should have known better than to compliment him. Sinking her teeth into his chest, she playfully nipped him, which earned her another swat on her bottom.

"Go to sleep woman, you're going to need your strength."

Chapter Twelve

Alexandra woke in the morning to find herself naked and alone in the big bed. She saw the late morning sun high in the sky through the window. The past night seemed like a dream, and what a dream it had been.• She'd had no idea how magical or wondrous things could be between a man and a woman. Her face flushed with embarrassment at the thought of the things they'd done during the night. How was she going to face Ian this morning? She reluctantly left the comfort of the warm bed and made her way across the cold floor to the basin of water left by the hearth. She hadn't heard anyone knock this morning. Hopefully, the furs had covered her naked body.

She was surprised by how stiff and tender she was. She hadn't noticed any pain after the first time they'd made love. Cleaning herself up, she dressed for the day in her usual working garb. What were her responsibilities as the laird's wife? No guards awaited her outside the door. Walking down to the main hall, she passed several servants who stopped to smile and ask how she was. Alexandra blushed each time she was asked, and managed to stutter out an answer. It was as if the entire clan knew exactly what had happened in the bedroom last night.

The main hall was empty. Everyone had already eaten and gone about their business. She hated to bother

Cook, but she was really hungry this morning since she'd not eaten much the night before. As she made her way into the kitchen area, the staff stopped talking and looked up in surprise. She asked if there was any left-over porridge from the morning's meal. Everyone answered at once and jumped up to serve her. Cook ushered her into a seat at the utility table. What had gotten into everybody? Was this how a laird's wife was always treated? Alexandra was grateful, but embarrassed to be fussed over. She was no different from any of them.

After she ate her breakfast, she decided to check in with Silas as usual. Walking briskly, she set a vigorous pace. The sun was brightly shining, but the air was colder than during the last few days. She saw no sign of young Jamie and Happy, and she prayed that they stayed out of danger. The McGregor was training with his men as usual. She slowed her pace to watch. Since he stood a head taller than most of his men, he was always easy to spot. Watching him, Alexandra once again felt her face overheating as she remembered their lovemaking. *Would she ever be able to stop blushing?*

Alexandra didn't find Silas in his hut, so she walked toward the other end of the village asking everyone she encountered if they'd seen him. As before, she was surprised when the people she met stopped what they were doing to inquire how she was, and if they could get her anything. Finally, she ran into someone who told her where Silas could be found.

As she approached the designated hut, she spotted Silas talking with one of her favorite guards. The guardsman, whose name she knew only as Mac, usually laughed and joked with all, but today he frowned and paced before Silas. She heard the old man explaining to him that first-time babies often took longer to get birthed. She heard Mac reply, "But it's not her time yet, and she's been laboring for over a day."

She walked up next to him and touched Mac's elbow. "I didn't know your wife was expecting. May I go in and see her?"

Mac, barely holding his composure, nodded.

Alexandra had never witnessed the birthing of a babe before. She stood back and watched with the other women. The girl's face was contorted in pain as she attempted to push with each contraction. The woman standing next to Alexandra whispered to her that the baby was in a breech position, and they had tried to get it to turn by moving Mary, the mother, into different angles. Time came and went, and the poor woman was losing her strength to push.

Alexandra moved up and sat beside the girl and held her hand, encouraging her as best she could. Silas had already said there was nothing he knew to do. The birthing of babes was strictly women's business.

She watched as the will to live drained from Mary. The other women gave each other knowing, sorrowful looks. Alexandra, sensing with panic that there was not much time left, decided she had to at least try to do something more. After washing her hands in hot soapy water, she approached the woman and explained she was going to reach inside her to turn the baby. Mary did not have the strength to answer but nodded her understanding and closed her eyes.

Thankfully, Alexandra had small hands, but the poor girl still cried out as she inserted her right hand. She could feel the babe's tiny feet. Pushing the babe back up the birthing canal was not easy. She worked with just her fingertips until she was able to turn the babe around and she could feel the softness of its hair. Alexandra pulled her hand free and each woman in the room loudly encouraged and cajoled the girl into pushing one last time.

The babe came out in a gush, and Alexandra caught the slippery little body in her hands. It was a boy, and he was unmoving. The umbilical cord was wrapped about his tiny neck. She quickly unwound it, and the babe's little chest began to rise and fall. He let out a pathetic cry, and his scrawny fists waved in the air. Alexandra turned and handed him to the nearest woman while she cut the cord that attached him to his mother.

As the women took care of the babe, Alexandra turned her attention back to the young mother. Mary had passed out, and she was bleeding heavily. Alexandra quickly packed clean rags into her womb. She turned to the other women for help, but they had no further ideas. She called Silas to the doorway and urgently asked his advice. He shook his head and sent in Mac. With tears streaming down his face, Mac gathered his young wife to his chest. Wretched sobs shook his body as she died in his arms.

Alexandra could not hold back her own tears as she watched. If only she knew more about birthing, she might have been able to save the woman. She turned to Silas, who'd entered the hut and was cleaning out the babe's mouth and nostrils.

"Will he live?" she whispered.

"Only time will tell if he is old enough to survive. His breathing is rapid, but his color is good."

"Is there someone who can nurse him?" she asked.

"Mary was Maddie's cousin. She comes from a big family. I've no doubt someone will volunteer to take the child until he is old enough for Mac to care for."

On hearing the news, Alexandra's eyes filled with tears again. She was sorry for the pain Maddie would feel.

She hated death, and she hated her own inadequacy to prevent it.

Stepping out of the hut, she was surprised to see the sun was setting. The hours had passed in a blur. She headed back to the keep at a fast pace, knowing the McGregor would be expecting her for dinner, though she had no appetite whatsoever. As she walked back, she recognized in the distance the McGregor's large form headed toward her. Her heart leapt at the sight of him.

****

Ian spotted Alexandra walking with her head lowered, watching the ground. He'd thought about her throughout the day, and he looked forward to their evening together. Instead of waiting at the keep, he'd set out to find her. As she drew closer and spotted him, her face lit up and her pace quickened. He was surprised when she threw herself into his arms at the last second. Lifting her face, he noted the dried tears and red eyes. He stepped back and took in her entire appearance. His eyes widened as he saw the blood on her gown. He was immediately concerned she had hurt herself. *He should have kept the guards with her*.

"Are you hurt?" he asked, frowning as he looked for a wound.

"No, no, I'm fine. It's not my blood." Her voice

cracked and she started crying again as she explained about the death of Mary.

Ian said nothing but pulled her back into his arms and held her while she cried. He also mourned the loss of a fellow clan member and he thought of Mac's grief.

****

Debra screamed in ecstasy as she faked her orgasm. She'd learned years ago the more she fed a man's ego, the easier he was to manipulate.

Robert finally climbed off her. "I'm on the schedule for the hunting party next week. Will you miss me when I'm gone?"

"No! Not so soon," she whined and moved to place her head on his chest. She ran her hands over his muscled chest before dipping lower to cup his manhood. "Then you better start making it up to me now."

Always planning ahead, she'd made a pattern of sporadically staying away from the keep for a day or two at a time. So, in the event she needed to be elsewhere, her absence wouldn't be noted. Robert was always unwittingly cooperative when she wanted to stay home at night, as she did tonight. She would say she "needed" him and compensate him with wanton sex over several days, before totally ignoring him again. He was big and dumb and predictably easy to control. Too bad he wasn't the laird.

****

Debra rode toward the Campbell stronghold. She'd been on the road since daybreak, leaving the hut shortly after Robert had left to join the hunting party. He'd be gone for no less than three days. She had been hatching this plan since he'd first mentioned his name would be coming up on the schedule. It should take her no more than one complete day to get to and from the Campbell stronghold. She didn't think anyone would miss her. She hadn't any friends who would miss her presence, nor did she want any.

She'd ridden in the same direction as the hunting party so her trail mingled with theirs, and she wore a plain, nondescript brown cloak pulled up over her head so even if she were noticed, her red hair wouldn't give her away. Once the village was out of sight, she veered north toward the Campbells' land. She should arrive shortly before dusk if all went well. And it had to go well.

The McGregors and the Campbells had been sworn enemies for over one hundred years, but they had not fought any major battles against one another in a decade. The degree of their fighting rose and fell. Things would be relatively quiet for a while and then one side stole the other's cows or horses, and the skirmishing broke out again, seeing which clan could best the other. It had almost turned into a game, albeit at times, a deadly one.

Debra planned to make the Campbell laird an offer he couldn't refuse. If she could just get in to see him, she was certain she could persuade him. Hopefully, he wouldn't be away on some stupid raid. She dug her heels into the sides of the sluggish horse to speed it up. Unfortunately, in her haste she hadn't considered food for herself or the horse. She only realized she was on Campbell land when she was suddenly surrounded by five men on horseback, each man armed and boasting the Campbell colors.

Slowly lowering her hood so they could see she

was a woman, Debra said, "I have an important message for your laird."

"Who are you? And who is the message from?" one of the older men barked out.

"I am Debra McCaw," she said, lifting her head high. "The message is from me. I am currently living with the McGregor clan, but I am a distant cousin of the Campbell laird. It is urgent that I speak with him. I have news he will want to hear."

The men looked to one another until one of them nodded. The man closest to her moved in and grabbed her reins, and she was led to the Campbell stronghold. Two men stayed with her while the others entered the keep. Debra noted everything while she waited. This keep was smaller than the McGregor's, and some of its walls were crumbling and in need of repair. Fewer merchant huts surrounded the structure, and the people she saw were not well-dressed, or well-bathed for that matter.

Beckoned, Debra slid off her horse and followed the men inside. The main hall was dark and smelled badly. She was led up to a table filled with men who paid little attention to her as they hungrily attacked their food. She decided to wait until her presence was acknowledged before speaking. Finally, an older man with long red hair and matching beard looked up from his food, long enough to glare at her.

He said loudly, "So we be cousins?"

Debra answered, "No, but I thought saying so might ensure my meeting you."

The man laughed before taking a slug of ale and wiping his mouth across his sleeve. "You have guts, I'll say that. Now what is this urgent message from the

McGregor?"

"It's not from the McGregor, it's from me. I know of a way you can make a lot of money and get the best of him." She paused to see the effect of her words.

"I'm listening." The laird turned his attention back to his food. The other men looked on with more interest as they finished up their meal.

"The McGregor holds a woman hostage for ransom. Her cousin Niles Conrad and her husband-to-be Hugh Sullivan are willing to pay handsomely for her return." Debra smirked and then added, "In any condition."

The Campbell laird scowled and said, "And how does that help me?"

"Don't you see, all you have to do is steal the woman from the McGregor and collect the ransom for yourself."

The man slammed his mug down on the table, sloshing its contents, and yelled, "You think stealing a woman from the McGregor will be easy?" He motioned with his hand for the men to take her away.

Debra spoke quickly, "I have a plan. She trusts me. I can get her to one of the outer village houses with only two guardsmen. You can leave evidence pointing the finger at Hugh Sullivan and her cousin. The McGregor will immediately suspect them anyway." Debra shouted this last part as a guard grabbed her arm and pulled her toward the door.

"Wait!" the Campbell laird ordered. "Bring her back." He paused, silently considering her words before he said, "Where are our manners? Come, sit and eat. Let us discuss the merits of this plan."

Chapter Thirteen

Alexandra could scarce believe she'd been living with the McGregor clan for over two months. The time had passed so quickly, and yet, it seemed like she'd known these people for years. Being part of a family again was wonderful. She was happy. There was no doubt about it. She was in love with Ian. She loved his strength and his gentleness. She loved his humor, and she loved his serious commitment as leader of his people. No place was so safe, so warm or so desirable as when she lay naked in his arms. Their lust for one another was undeniable, and they couldn't keep their hands off each other. All it took was a simple, innocent touch to ignite a flame. She felt totally fulfilled. Perhaps this had been God's plan all along, that she be the Wolf's wife and help care for his people. She wished she knew the depth of Ian's feelings. They shared their bodies and their stories, but he seemed to withhold a part of himself.

She walked the well-worn path to Silas's house deep in thought. Jamie and Happy ran ahead but were still within her sights. The wolf pup had grown much during these past two months and although they'd managed to teach him some manners, for the most part, he did exactly what he wanted.

The beauty of the day matched her mood as she strolled along the drying path. The foliage was coming back to life. Trees were budding and the grass was turning from brown to green. The sun blessed her with its warmth. She felt like lifting her arms out to her sides and twirling around as a child would, with her face lifted toward the sun. So she did. She was carefree this morning, due partly she was sure, to the fact she no longer had guards tagging along behind her. The McGregor had succumbed to her renewed wishes to roam freely, but only as long as she stayed within the confines of the village.

Jamie ran back down the path and skidded to a halt in front of her. "Race you to the door!" he exclaimed with a flushed face. Without waiting for a response, he turned and ran.

Alexandra laughed and picked up her skirts and sprinted after him. The excited wolf pup ran back and forth between them, yipping and grabbing at their heels. Jamie was the first to arrive at Silas's door and slammed into it. Alexandra followed seconds behind.

"I win!" Jamie proclaimed.

"So you did, fair and square," she puffed out between gulps of air. Leaning heavily against the door, she was almost knocked off her feet when it suddenly swung open behind her.

"What the devil's going on out here?" Silas shouted irritably.

Alexandra and Jamie grinned at one another like co-conspirators before Alexandra answered, "Just a little spring fever going around."

"Well, stop it! We've work to do," he grumbled and moved aside to let them in.

Silas was adamant it was a perfect day to hunt for a herb he called wild garlic. He said the leaves from this plant could make a tea for intestinal disorders. He further explained there was a very short window of opportunity for finding the plant for it was rare and only found in the spring. Most years, he said, he came back from his search empty-handed. Perfect weather conditions needed to be followed by extreme luck, and today Silas felt lucky.

Alexandra agreed to accompany him on his hunt. Young Jamie declined the offer to help, stating he was going to go play with his new friends, Bryce and Brian McDouglas. They were rambunctious twins who were several years older, but the trio got along well. Alexandra was happy to see Jamie make friends, and even better, Mrs. McDouglas kept an eagle eye on her boys.

Alexandra helped Silas gather empty containers, load the bags, and sling them over his horse's back. The old nag was a sweet girl. They wouldn't be riding her, but she'd carry their load.

"I need to tell the McGregor I'm leaving the village," she said as they finished up.

"We're going to be within sight of the keep. I'm not going to waste precious time waiting for you. Either come now or don't bother."

She considered her options. The McGregor wouldn't be happy, but they wouldn't be far, and she wouldn't be alone. The deciding factor was she didn't want Silas to be outside the perimeter by himself.

"Okay, let's get moving," she said and gathered the horse's reins and waited for Silas to lead the way.

The day was lovely she thought, if you could ignore the grumblings of an old man. With each hour that passed, Silas became more anxious in his pursuit of wild garlic. They scanned the perimeter wall of the village looking mainly at the base of trees. Brushing dead leaves away with their boots, they looked for the attractive white flower. Alexandra concluded their endeavor was akin to looking for a needle in a haystack, and it would only be by a stroke of good luck that they stumbled across this precious plant.

"I found some by the west creek once where it flows through a meadow. Wild garlic grew on the south side in bunches. I'd never seen so much all in one place, especially out in the open like that. I went back every year for at least ten years but never found it again," Silas reminisced. "I think we should try the creek again. It's been a few years since I last searched there," he said.

"How far is it?" Alexandra asked, concerned about the amount of daylight left.

"I'd say an hour there and back. Plenty of time," he said and turned away from the village to head deeper into the forest.

Leading the horse, she trailed closely behind. The deeper they moved into the trees, the less sunlight shone through the branches. A muffled stillness engulfed them, broken below by the rustling of leaves as they walked through them, and above by the occasional call of a bird.

She had plenty of time to think as they walked, and she started to feel a touch anxious about the McGregor's reaction to her leaving the village. Hopefully, he hadn't noticed her absence. If so, she would be tempted not to mention it. But no, that didn't feel right. She would confess her folly and attempt to explain herself. Her guards would undoubtedly be guarding her backside again tomorrow.

They walked on and on. Alexandra stopped now and again to give the nag a handful of grain and to stroke her neck. After what she determined to be at least an hour, she called ahead to Silas, "How much farther? We should probably head back soon."

Silas stopped and looked around as if to get his bearings, "We're almost to the creek. Any time now," he said and trudged off in a slightly different direction.

Where did he find the energy? She hoped if she were lucky enough to make it to old age, she would be as agile and tireless, albeit less curmudgeonly. More time passed and they still had not come to the creek.

Puzzled, Silas said, "I don't understand. It should be here." He squinted into the trees in every direction.

"We can try again another day. Silas..." she paused, waiting until she had his full attention. "We must head back," she said, emphasizing each word.

Silas sighed in defeat. "Aye."

Unfortunately, turning back turned out not to be an easy thing. She'd been deep in her own thoughts when they journeyed in, paying but the slightest attention to her surroundings. The trees all looked the same. Apparently, they did to Silas also, as he stopped and muttered under his breath every few minutes before leading them onward.

Alexandra controlled her rising anger when she realized they were lost. She was mad at herself, and she was mad at him. How could she be so stupid? She should have never left the village. What was she thinking? And Silas? He needed to admit he was an old man with failing eyesight who should know his limitations.

Trying to remain calm, she said impatiently, "We need to find shelter. It will be dark soon."

Silas said nothing. Not meeting her eyes, he nodded in agreement.

Daylight dwindled. There was not much shelter to be found and not enough time to construct one. They settled on the hollowed out base of an ancient, dying tree. It would be snug, but with their backs against the inner wall, there was enough room to get the upper half of their bodies out of the elements. Alexandra tethered the horse and fed her the last of the grain. Thankfully, they'd also brought water for the nag and themselves. Both she and Silas drank a small amount before giving the horse what remained.

As the last bits of light faded away, they wedged into the tree. Their shared body warmth would help a little. Silas had not worn a jacket, but Alexandra had the thin shawl she'd worn that morning, and she spread it over their legs. They listened in silence to the darkness before Alexandra said, "The McGregor's going to kill us."

"Aye, he is," Silas returned. After several more minutes of silence, he added, "I'm sorry, lass. I'm such an old fool."

Alexandra's anger melted away. She took his weathered hand in hers and said, "We are both fools."

****

Laughing, Ian jumped up from the ground and gave his brother a hearty hug, slapping him on the back.

"You've been practicing," he said.

"No, you just have your mind elsewhere. I dare to say it's on visions of a naked, golden-haired wife?" James teased.

The McGregor tossed a fist into James's right shoulder that would have knocked a smaller man off his feet. Still smiling, he said, "Mind your own business."

Ian called off practice for the day and headed to the keep to clean up. His thoughts had most definitely been on his wife. She was like an intoxicating drug. The more he had her the more he wanted. Much more.

She wasn't in their bedchamber when he returned, but that was not unusual as tending the sick sometimes went into the night. He cleaned up at the basin and donned fresher, less offensive clothes. He'd have a drink with the men while he waited.

Not as many clan members gathered in the meeting hall tonight. No doubt they were enjoying the last bits of the unusually warm day. James shared a small table with Jamie, and Ian watched them play a match of chess. His nephew was surprisingly good at it. Since Alexandra had taught Jamie how to play, he improved with each game. Ian watched the boy focus intently on his next move. He waited until it was his brother's turn and asked the boy if he knew who his wife was healing.

"I haven't seen her since this morning." Wrinkling his nose to show his disinterest, he said, "They were going to find some plant."

Ian felt the first spark of concern. "Did they take Silas's horse?"

Not taking his eyes off the board as it was his turn, the lad nodded yes.

James looked up from the game and met his brother's dark eyes. "I'll gather some men," he said and stood.

Within minutes, a group of ten, including the McGregor and his brother, met on horseback in front of

Silas's hut. The home sat empty, and Silas's horse was missing. Mere minutes of daylight remained. The McGregor split his men up and scattered them along the outside of the village wall. With orders to work in a pattern out from the wall toward the forest, they combed the ground looking for any sign.

A sharp whistle and wave from a warrior on the west side of the wall gained everyone's attention and the rest of the group galloped over to him. McGregor jumped from his horse before it came to a complete stop and examined the ground. Yes, there were tracks of two light-weight people and a horse. He followed the trail until it disappeared into the edge of the forest. He would have gone farther except his brother's horse appeared to block his path.

"We cannot track them in the dark. You'll lose it, and waste precious time in the morning coming back to find where it begins again," James reasoned.

Ian knew his brother spoke the truth, but he barely contained himself from running in after her. Jaw clenched, he nodded to James.

James took command and shouted, "Everyone meet back here before the break of day."

The brothers rode back to the keep in silence. In the main hall, warriors and servants whispered among themselves, shooting wary glances at the Wolf and giving him wide berth. James said something quietly to his son, and Jamie rose without protest and left the room.

Teeth clenched, Ian nursed his ale and glared into the fire. It was early spring, but the night air was still considerably cold. Was she freezing? His fear and his anger battled for victory. She had wantonly disobeyed him! Had the woman no sense? He wanted to throttle her or better yet, turn her over his knee and give her the spanking of her life. If she was still alive. His gut clenched as he thought of the many dangers they might have encountered. Predators of the two-legged as well as the four-legged variety. The McGregor held up his mug, signaling for more ale. It was going to be a long night. There would be no sleep.

****

Alexandra heard her own and Silas's teeth chattering. Huddled side-by-side, his bony elbow dug uncomfortably into her ribs whenever he moved, but at least they were getting warmth from one another. Thank God there was some shelter from the wind. She periodically stomped her feet and wiggled her toes when they began to feel numb. She thought she heard an owl, or at least, she hoped it was an owl. The night was pitch black. Clouds must have moved in, covering the glow of the moon. As she grew attuned to the forest sounds, thoughts of the McGregor and their next meeting plagued her. She pulled the wolf ring out from its resting place between her breasts and fiddled with it. How mad was he going to be? A crawling sensation tickled the back of her neck and she quickly brushed it away. She shivered, but not from the cold. It was going to be one abominably long night.

****

Morning came with the far off sound of rolling thunder. Rain was coming. She could feel it in the air. Silas agreed it would be best to stay where they had shelter. Neither doubted the McGregor would find them, and it would happen faster if he didn't have to track them all over the countryside. The storm moved closer and louder, and at first she mistook the galloping sound of horses' hooves for thunder until she heard the jangle of riding gear and the neighing and snorting of horses. The warriors formed a half circle before the opening in the tree with McGregor seated at the center of the group on his black stallion. No one spoke, as first, Silas stiffly unfolded himself out the narrow opening, followed by a more limber Alexandra. Eyes downcast, they stood before the warriors like two ashamed, scolded children.

She looked up and searched the McGregor's face. One millisecond of a glance was all it took to know she was in big trouble. His dark eyes were furious. She had never seen this level of anger in him, let alone directed at her. He turned and said something to his brother, something she did not hear, and James prodded his horse closer and stretched out his hand for Silas. Once Silas was seated behind James, the warriors turned and trotted off, leaving her alone with the McGregor.

Still glaring furiously at her, the McGregor thrust out his hand for her to accept, almost as if he dared her to take it. Thunder rolled around them and shook the ground. Her face heated with embarrassment and rising anger. She lifted her head and strode toward him while thinking of the horrible night she'd just endured and how he didn't have to be such a beast about it. Without breaking stride, she slapped her hand into his. She was airborne before she knew it, almost slung completely over the horse to the other side. She grabbed his waist to keep from falling and had barely righted herself before the McGregor kicked the horse into a gallop.

Just as Alexandra worried their pace might kill the horse, the McGregor pulled up in front of a hunter's cabin. So they'd not been far from real shelter last night, she thought and slid from the horse not waiting to see whether the McGregor would offer assistance. Not looking at her, he walked the horse under the lean-to and gave him food and water.

She stood in the open and watched the McGregor as lightning cracked across one end of the sky to the other, chased by the booming claps of thunder. A deluge of rain fell from the heavens. She didn't move. She'd rather face him out here in the open and get it over with.

She waited as the McGregor finished providing for his horse and turned to dash into the cabin. He stopped abruptly when he noticed her and stood unmoving, just staring. With a loud roar, he ran full-out straight toward her. Her heart stopped and she froze a second before stepping back. He was on her in an instant. She heard herself involuntarily scream as she was hoisted over his shoulder. She was still screaming when he burst through the cabin door and tossed her onto a pile of straw. She immediately sprang back up and faced him with fists clenched. Her heart raced with fear and anger.

"Does your word mean nothing?" he roared, towering over her.

Alexandra struggled for something to say.

"Have you so little respect for me, you defy me in front of my whole clan?" he yelled, incredulous.

Tears gathered in her eyes. She released her fists and let the fight drain out of her.

"I am so sorry," she said and looked up into his eyes, hoping he could see she genuinely meant it. "You are right. I have no excuses to give." She spread her hands wide. "I didn't think it through, and I made a bad choice, but I truly didn't mean to disrespect you in front of your people." Tears rolled down her face, and she swiped them away in embarrassment. She swallowed, "I deserve whatever punishment you see fit."

He wrapped a hand around each upper arm and yanked her full against him.

"You deserve to be beaten," he whispered, staring into her upturned face. She waited, holding her breath, as conflicting emotions crossed his. She knew she must look like a drowned rat with tears and raindrops falling down her cheeks. Finally, the anger faded from his face and he wrapped his arms around her and crushed her against him, bending to ravage her mouth.

Alexandra could barely breathe. He held her so tight, yet she didn't want to move. This was where she wanted to be. Ian's tongue plunged into her mouth and she kissed him back with everything she had. When he started removing her wet clothes, she murmured in agreement and urgently began undressing him. Garments were strewn across the pile of straw until only her chemise remained on. Ian pushed her backward and fell with her onto the mound of hay. Ceaselessly kissing her, he slid the chemise up over her hips and lifted them up, driving deep and hard into her. Alexandra moaned as his fullness stretched her taut. Moving in and out, he plunged deeper and deeper, taking her higher and higher with each thrust. She reached the pinnacle first and was floating on waves of release when she felt Ian's tension leave him. She clung to him and took his full weight as he went slack.

****

Alexandra woke to find herself spooned tightly in front of Ian and with his arm wrapped about her waist.

He lifted the hair from the nape of her neck and gently placed kisses down to her shoulder. His warm breath and tongue caressed her skin, leaving goose bumps in its wake. She felt him grow between her thighs, below her buttocks. She enjoyed the languid feel of her body as she lay totally relaxed, enjoying the feelings he provoked. When he squeezed her breast and then teased her nipple by rubbing his rough thumb across its tip before tugging and pulling it, she moaned in awakening excitement.

Ian rolled over onto his back, turning her with him as he did, until she lay on top of him. He cupped her thighs below her buttocks and pulled her forward until he was in position. Releasing her only to grab her hips, he slid her along the outside of his manhood. He lifted her up and thrust upward as he pulled her down. Alexandra gasped in shock and moved her hands to cover his before she gave in to the wondrous sensation he created as he taught her how to love him.

Chapter Fourteen

Rain fell throughout the morn and into the afternoon. Alexandra lay in Ian's arms and listened to the distant rumblings and the patter of rain on the cabin's roof. They talked, they slept, and they explored each other's bodies. Alexandra brought up a subject she'd avoided since their marriage.

"What will you do when my cousin sends a messenger that the ransom is ready?"

"I have not fully decided. I want revenge, but I am not willing to lose any of my men for that pig. I may meet him at the designated place and challenge him to a personal fight, though I don't see him brave enough to accept such a challenge."

"Please be careful," Alexandra pleaded. "He is pure evil and stops at nothing to get what he wants. You cannot believe a word that comes out of his mouth. He will be plotting to trick or ambush you."

"Aye, I imagine so. James and I have not decided which path we will choose, but you should not give the man any more thought. He is my concern now," he said with a grisly smile. "Besides, you have more important duties, like learning how to please your new husband," he said arrogantly.

"Really? Like this?" She poked him under the armpit where she had discovered he was ticklish and started exploring to find all of his ticklish spots.

Laughing, he pulled away whilst grabbing her hands and wrestling her underneath him. Holding her hands above her head, he gave her a lingering kiss and declared it was time to head back to the keep.

The ride back to the stronghold was a slow one. The forest floor was muddy and treacherous for the horse, and the McGregor let him pick his gait. Alexandra spent the majority of the ride pulling pieces of embedded straw from her hair. When they arrived at the keep, the McGregor ordered water for a shared bath.

Walking down the stairs by herself for evening meal, she was reminded of the first time she'd walked down them. From the top of the stairs, she heard a clamor of laughter, shouting and music. By the time she reached the bottom step, only hushed silence remained. The McGregor stood, smiled, and reached out his hand to her. Immediately, the talking and festivities resumed. The clansmen were polite with their stares, sneaking glances between their activities. Some were curious, some were sympathetic, but a few were hostile. She was sure they were all wondering the same thing. Did he beat her?

When she sat down, James nodded and smiled at her. Young Jamie was solemn, his brown eyes like saucers. "Were you scared?" he asked.

Alexandra leaned forward and raised her eyebrows to emphasize her answer. "Very!"

"I should have gone with you. I could have helped protect you."

The men grinned between their bites of food. Alexandra's heart was touched. He was so adorable. "You are the best nephew ever! I'm sure I would have been less scared had you been there."

Happy rose from the boy's feet and sat by her side, resting his head upon her lap. This was something new. She stroked his head, and he did not move. He either missed her company, or he wanted some of her food.

****

From across the room Debra watched, making sure to plant a sympathetic look on her face. She burned with envy. She should be sitting at the head table by now, wearing pretty clothes and having pretty things, being waited on hand and foot. She had hoped Alexandra would have met some ill fate during her night in the forest, and if not, she had derived pleasure from the thought the McGregor would beat her soundly. But no, that was obviously not the case, the woman was practically glowing.

Debra burned with memories of her own beatings. Whippings as a child for stealing food or avoiding work, and again as a woman when caught stealing money from a drunkard who'd "paid" for her services. She'd received more than her fair share. This Englishwoman needed to feel the sting of the lash. She took comfort in knowing the woman wouldn't be glowing for long.

****

Alexandra woke abruptly, her heart pounding. She'd had yet another nightmare. Feeling bile rise up in her throat, she scampered out of bed to the chamber pot and vomited. Her face was sweaty and her breathing heavy. She leaned a hand against the wall and waited to see if there would be a second wave, but the nausea passed.

The nightmares were occurring more frequently, and she believed they were due to waiting for Niles's messenger to arrive. Each day that went by increased the likelihood the courier would show up on the next. The stress was making her ill. She did not know what Ian was planning, but he worked his men harder than ever. In the evenings, as she played chess with Jamie, Ian and James huddled over maps and quietly planned their own strategies.

Forcing her mind to more pleasant thoughts, she dressed and headed to Silas's. She had no idea what the day had in store. They had found the wild garlic with the help of her guards. One of the clansmen knew exactly where the meadow Silas had referred to could be found.

She arrived at Silas's to find him immersed in cataloging the herbs they had collected over the last week. The interior of his hut was dark in contrast to the morning sunshine, and it stank of fish. Alexandra's stomach rolled again and she pinched her nose.

"Have you been cooking fish?" she asked and held her breath.

"Aye, trout and onions," Silas replied, looking up from his work. He noted her green color and pointed to a pot in the corner.

Gagging, with her hand over her mouth, she rushed to the pot just in time to lose the contents of her stomach. Silas handed her a cool, wet cloth.

She wiped her mouth and apologized in embarrassment, "I'm sorry about that. I've not been feeling well lately. I probably should have stayed in my bedchamber."

Silas gave her a queer, knowing look. "Are you with child?"

Dear God, she hadn't even considered the

possibility. Silas pulled out a chair, and she immediately sank down on it and lowered her head between her legs. Could it be? So soon? When the nausea passed, she leaned back in the chair and placed her hands over her stomach.

"I don't know," she said in wonderment.

"Something to consider. Why don't you take it easy today? I have no need of your assistance at the moment," he said and stooped over his project.

Alexandra agreed and was grateful to be back out in the fresh air. Not ready to return to the keep, she decided on a long walk to the end of the village. With her guards not far behind, she walked on, lost in her thoughts.

A babe. She was filled with emotions at the thought. Overwhelmed, overjoyed, scared, awed. She pictured a healthy son in her arms with thick brown hair and dark eyes, and with dimples. Chubby and cooing. Then she envisioned the McGregor cradling a toddler daughter with curling blonde hair. Her eyes grew misty. When had she had her last menses? She couldn't remember. Would the McGregor be happy? He should be, as that was his reason for marrying her.

She was shaken from her thoughts when she saw Debra running toward her. The woman reached her and stopped to catch her breath before she could talk. Bending over and placing her hands on her knees, she took a few wheezing gasps and said, "There's something wrong with Robert. Please come quickly?"

"What is it?" Alexandra placed a reassuring hand on the woman's back.

"I don't know. He was eating and then all of a sudden, he fell to the ground, stiff and jerking. Please hurry!" Debra said and turned to run, looking back to make sure Alexandra was following.

They were at the east end of the village, and Debra led them through the east gate and toward the forest. Alexandra knew several families lived outside the village walls, but she had not been to any of their homes. With her guards following closely, she ran after Debra, who ran surprisingly fast. No wonder she'd been out of breath. She must really love this Robert of hers.

A hut came into view, and Debra disappeared into it. Alexandra entered shortly behind her. The interior was dark and she waited for her eyes to adjust. A man lay unmoving on the floor beside the table. Alexandra darted forward and knelt next to him. It was quickly apparent he was already dead. His open, unmoving eyes were fixed upon the ceiling. Dread filled Alexandra's heart, and she turned back to inform Debra.

****

Alexandra thought she was dreaming of the past when she awoke. She dreamt she was tethered to a horse once again and hanging upside down with a gag in her mouth, waiting for the McGregor to come rescue her. It took several moments to realize she was not having a nightmare, but was living one.

The trotting of the horse beat steadily against her stomach. Bile rose in her mouth behind the gag, and she managed to swallow it. Thank God, her stomach was empty and nothing was left to throw-up, or she might drown in her own vomit. A blanket or a bag of some sort covered her head. How did she get here? She remembered seeing an explosion of light and feeling sharp pain at the back of the head, and then nothing, until now.

Alexandra trembled in fear. This had to be Niles's doing. No wonder they hadn't received word from a messenger. He'd probably been planning to abduct her all along. How much time did she have before they reached him? Would he meet her captors or was she being taken all the way back to the estate? Questions chased each other in her head. Tears welled up as she thought of the babe in her stomach. Would he survive if Niles gave her a brutal beating? She calmed herself with thoughts of the McGregor. He would find her. She just had to keep her wits until he did. She prayed for safety for herself and her unborn child.

Listening to the sounds around her, she determined there were only four to five captors. They talked little and moved swiftly. At one point, they stopped briefly, only long enough to change horses before moving on at an even swifter pace. When her abductors untied her and moved her to a fresh horse, she remained limp and unmoving in hopes they would think she was still unconscious. And she wasn't far from it, the pain in her head was excruciating. Hanging upside down with blood rushing to her head wasn't helping any. She'd already swallowed her vomit several times, and she was afraid of what might happen if she were to fall unconscious.

She tugged at the tether around her wrists. She couldn't tell if it were leather or rope. If it were leather, she might be able to stretch it wide enough to pull one hand out. The pain she was causing her wrists helped her to ignore the pain in her head. The bindings chafed and tore her skin as she worked at loosening them.

****

Ian was pleased with his men. They'd trained for

long, hard hours over the past months and it showed, not that they'd been in bad shape to start. With pride, he knew each warrior had reached his potential. Together, they were a force to be feared. The younger lads lined up daily and watched their training with envy, eager to join. When Niles and Sullivan were defeated, he'd start the process of grooming the next group of boys to join their ranks.

James had already informed the men there would be no extra training this night. The evening was theirs to enjoy. They'd earned it. Some of the men headed for the main hall whooping and hollering, while others left to be with their families. As he walked back to the keep with his brother, Ian kept a watchful eye out for his wife. He had not seen her since the morn.

The merry-making started earlier than usual, before the nightly meal was presented. He knew it was a way for the men to release the tensions that were building. Tensions from knowing a fight was brewing, and waiting for it to begin. His warriors knew better than to get drunk, as they could be called upon to draw arms at a moment's notice.

There was still no sign of his wife. However, the two men who'd been assigned to guard her were also absent. Walking among the tables, he inquired at the different groups if anyone knew who his wife was healing. After he circled the tables once, he stopped back at his seat. He picked up his pewter plate in one hand and his spoon in the other and beat on the plate until the room quieted and he had everyone's attention.

"Has anyone," he shouted, "seen my wife since this morning?"

Complete silence ensued as everyone looked

around the room. With exasperation, the McGregor bellowed the order, "Search the village!"

His men immediately rose to their feet. He made eye contact with his brother and nodded for him to take command. James gave instructions, dividing them into search parties and directing them to meet back in the center of the village. Though not instructed to do so, most of the women and children joined in to help.

The McGregor and James searched together. Young Jamie, who'd begged to help, tagged along behind. The McGregor consoled himself with the fact her guards were good men who wouldn't allow Alexandra to do anything foolish, nor would they be cajoled by her charms knowing they'd answer to him.

"Am I going to spend half of my life looking for this woman?" he wryly asked his brother as they searched.

"I'd say aye. Probably. But I imagine she's worth it," James answered with amusement.

****

Darkness had fallen by the time everyone met back up. Several torches were lit and passed out. The last of the search parties came in shaking their heads.

The McGregor shouted to be heard, "Has anyone noticed someone else absent or missing, today or this evening?"

Several names were mentioned, mainly elderly clan members who lived outside the village, and then someone shouted out, "Robert and Debra."

Ordering the women and children to go back to the keep or to their homes, Ian divided his men to search the outlying homes, starting with the homes of those declared missing. He announced which direction his group was headed so he could be easily found.

He chose to head for Robert's for two reasons. First, it was not too far and he wanted to stay as close to the center of the search as possible, and secondly, that was the direction his instinct told him to go. Moonlight made the path to Robert's easy to follow. No light glowed from within the hut as his party approached. They dismounted and re-lit the torches. The crumpled bodies of his guards lay on the ground.

Ian controlled his emotions and quickly examined the bodies. Ambushed. Both men had multiple back wounds. The young guard, Angus, had been completely caught off guard and bludgeoned from behind. The older one, McFearson, had some defensive wounds, but he had been overpowered.

Called into the hut, he entered to see his men untying the woman Debra, who was roped and gagged. The right side of her face was swollen and bruised. Dried blood from her nose covered her chin and stained the front of her dress. They examined the body of Robert, dead on the floor, but found no apparent wounds. Ian had no idea how he died.

As soon as the woman was untied, she threw herself over Robert's body. Sobbing and wailing with grief, she ignored Ian's attempts to question her.

"Where is Alexandra? Where is my wife?" he asked with growing impatience.

Before he could grab the woman and shake her, his brother halted him by grabbing his arm and opening his fist to reveal a torn piece of fabric, the Sullivan plaid.

Chapter Fifteen

Hours had passed since she'd started working on her restraints. Blood trickled down over her fingertips, making them slippery and the knots harder to handle.

Alexandra heard the horses come to a halt, followed by the sounds of dismounting. The binding that connected her bound hands to her bound feet must have been cut because she found herself slipping down the horse's side. Her feet hit the ground first, but caught off-balance, she landed on her backside. The binding around her ankles was severed, and she gasped in pain as blood flowed freely back into her feet. Pulled to a standing position by someone at each side, she was led with the hood still covering her head. She stumbled on numb feet and tried to keep up with her captors.

She didn't know where she was being steered, but she could tell they'd entered a building by the change in temperature and the echoes. Congratulatory greetings rang out. She heard laughter and loud talk. She smelled roasting meat, but her stomach didn't recoil. Suddenly released, she stumbled to a halt, disoriented and swaying to keep her balance.

"Well, let's have a look at her!" she heard a booming voice say.

The hood was roughly removed from her head, and she squinted at the change in light. The room grew silent, and people turned to stare at her. She stood at a table before a grizzly-looking man with long, graying, red hair, and an unpleasant, mean-looking face.

"So this is the woman worth all that money," the man drawled while looking her over. "Skinny little bitch. Don't look like good breeding stock to me!" he declared to the group, who guffawed and pounded the tables with their mugs.

Alexandra wouldn't have responded, even if she could have, as the gag was still in her mouth.

"Put her in the dungeon," he said with a dismissive wave of his hand. "No one's to touch her! She'll be worth more money to us! If they were willing to take her back in any condition, then they should be willing to pay extra if she's left untouched."

Relief flowed through Alexandra. She was amazed Niles's words had been so misconstrued. Led away and down a flight of stairs to a very dark place, she was shoved through a doorway, and the door slammed shut behind her. She heard the slide of a wooden bar lock into place. It took several minutes for her eyes to adjust again. A single beam of sunlight came in from a small rectangular window near the ceiling. The stench in the room was almost unbearable, and she gagged before realizing she still had the cloth over her mouth. Reaching up with her bound hands, she pulled it free.

A moan emanated from the darkest corner of the room. Alexandra walked hesitantly toward it. When she got closer, she could make out a boy lying face down in the straw. His back was bloody and crisscross swaths of his shirt were missing. It looked like he had been whiplashed. She placed her hand gently on his shoulder, and the lad shrank away from her in terror, turning partially over as he did so. He held his hands palms outward to keep her at bay. Why, it wasn't a boy at all. It was a woman! Her beautiful features were strikingly feminine, but her hair had been haphazardly shorn off, and it stuck out in uneven spikes.

"It's okay. It's okay," Alexandra repeated, taking a step back and raising her own hands, "I am not going to hurt you."

The young woman looked at her with glazed eyes. Alexandra was concerned she was running a fever.

"I just want to help," Alexandra said.

The woman did not answer but put her hands down and rolled back over onto her stomach, emitting a strangled cry as she did.

Alexandra walked closer and kneeled to get a better look. She needed more light. She did not want to pull the woman's shirt up without having any soothing ointment to apply. It looked like parts of the shirt were embedded in the open wounds, probably forced in by the whip. Fury rose up in her. The cruelty of some people never ceased to astonish her. She stood and walked to the door and started beating on it with her bound hands.

"I need help for this girl. or she could die if left untreated! Do you hear me? I need my medicinal supplies!" She'd had her healing bag strapped around her neck and at her side as usual when she was taken, surely they'd kept it. "And your laird has made a huge mistake! I need to talk to him!"

Alexandra continued to beat on the door and yell. She paused only long enough to bite at the knots in the rope binding her hands. Finally free, she shook her hands and examined them. They also needed healing salve. She determined as long as there was breath left in her, she'd stand at the door shouting and pounding until she dropped.

Eventually, after what seemed like hours, her medicinal bag was shoved through the sliding slot in the door.

"I need light! And I need to see your laird!" she yelled through the door, but received only silence in response.

She picked up her bag and took it to the section of the room where the last lingering rays of the day shone down through the rectangular window. It didn't look like anything was missing, but it had been rifled through. She found the herb she needed and went back by the door where she'd earlier discovered a water barrel and plate of uneaten stale bread. Setting the bread aside, she made a paste on the plate with the powdered medicine and a little water.

She walked over to where the woman lay unmoving and set the plate down on the straw. She pulled the hem of her undergarment up to her mouth and used her teeth to start a tear, and then with her hands, started pulling long strips of cloth off the bottom of her chemise. With nowhere clean to set them, she wrapped each strip around her left arm as she tore one off.

When she thought she had enough bandages, she knelt next to the woman.

"Are you awake?" she asked.

The woman lifted her head and turned in Alexandra's direction. Grimacing, she answered, "Yes."

Alexandra carefully explained what needed to be done and how painful the process would be, and then she waited for the woman's response.

Meeting her eyes unwaveringly, the woman nodded her head and whispered, "Please."

Alexandra worked quickly, as the remaining light was fading fast. Gently inching the shirt up, she was relieved to see the woman's back was not as bad as she'd first feared. Only several lashes had broken through her skin and those had bled heavily, causing the shirt to be caked in blood. The gashes were deep and she started the painful process of pulling the shredded remnants of clothing from them. The woman clenched fistfuls of straw, trying to hold back the screams, until she couldn't take it anymore. She let out a piercing cry and passed out.

It was hard to work with tears filling her eyes and running down her face, but Alexandra worked mainly by instinct anyway. Applying a generous amount of healing salve, she quickly wrapped the strips of garment over and around the unconscious woman's body.

Sinking to the ground when the job was done, she was overcome with weariness, almost too exhausted to tend to herself. She wiped what was left of the salve onto her wrists and covered them with the remaining strips. She was so very tired but hated to lie in the filth around her. Finally, she reconciled herself to the fact she had no choice. She needed all the rest she could get. Lying down on her side, she curled into a fetal position and rested her head on her folded arms. She would sleep until she heard the woman stir, and then go back to pounding on the door.

****

The McGregor waited in darkness for dawn to

approach. His clan was ready for war. They had prepared their provisions, their weapons, and their horses. By first light, they would be on the ambushers' trail, which undoubtedly led south toward the Conrad or Sullivan border.

A quarter of his men would stay behind under James's command to defend their home against attack. It was a rare decision to make, but they both agreed. The cunning treachery of Niles could not be underestimated. Coming onto his land and stealing his wife was proof of that.

The McGregor clenched his fists at the thought of Alexandra back in the bastard's hands. He hoped she realized she needed to keep silent regarding her marital status; elsewise, Niles would have no reason to keep her alive. If harm came to her, he would not stop until he tore the man apart, piece by piece.

The biggest obstacle to overcome in the upcoming battle was his own emotions. He needed to put a damper on his fury in order to think clearly. He would save Alexandra first and then he'd allow his feelings to run berserk.

****

Anguished cries woke Alexandra from her own nightmares. She reached out and squeezed the woman's hand to reassure her she was not alone.

"Can I please have some water?" the woman pushed herself up into a sitting position.

"Of course," Alexandra replied. She ran her hand along the wall to help guide her way. Moonlight now shone through the small window offering a reprieve from total darkness. She dipped the cup into the water barrel and also picked up the stale bread. Returning in the same manner, she held out the cup toward the woman's shadowed outline.

"Here it is," she said, waiting until she felt the woman's hand over hers before she let go of the tin cup. Splitting the bread in half, she encouraged her patient to eat to keep up her strength.

Alexandra took a bite and wanted to spit it out. Instead, she let it sit in her mouth until it softened enough to be swallowed. They sat eating in silence until Alexandra asked, "May I ask your name?"

"Kathleen or Kat for short. And yours?"

"Alexandra. Who did this to you?"

Kat hesitated and then stated without emotion, "My father."

Alexandra gasped. It was not the answer she expected. "I am so sorry," she said as visions of her own father played out in her head. Scenes of him laughing and tossing her up in the air to catch her again; of his kissing a scrape on her hand and making it magically better; of teaching her to ride and hunt. At a loss for words, she said again, "I am so sorry."

"And you? You are the woman who is being ransomed? I heard they were going to steal you from the McGregor clan."

"Yes, only there's just one problem—I am a McGregor now," Alexandra replied.

It took a second for Kat to register the meaning behind Alexandra's words, and then she chuckled before laughing outright. Wiping tears from her eyes, she said, "It serves the old bastard right."

Alexandra worked her way back to the door and pounded on it. She yelled again that she had an important message for the laird and beat on the door with her closed fists. She stopped banging long enough to ask Kat if she wanted more water.

"No, but will you please come talk to me more. Talk about anything, it keeps my mind off my pain."

Alexandra talked about her parents dying and Niles taking over their estate. She talked of his brutality and then about her ideal life at the nunnery. She paused to take a drink and said, "Tell me about your life."

"I am the youngest of nine children, and the only daughter. I had a different mother from my brothers. Theirs died in childbirth. Most of my childhood was spent trying to keep up with them," she said. "I learned how to fight, quick and dirty, as I can't match their strength, but I can outride them and outshoot them. I used to try so hard to gain my father's approval, but it was as if I were invisible. When I was old enough to understand, I found out my father killed my mother and her lover when he caught them cheating. People have told me I look like her. I think when my father looks at me he sees her," Kat stopped talking, overcome with emotion and unable to continue.

Alexandra squeezed her hand in sympathy. "Why don't you rest a while," she said and rose to pound again on the door. If there was anyone out there, they wouldn't be getting any more sleep than she did.

"Tell me how you met the McGregor," Kat requested, and turned to lie on her stomach.

Leaning back against the door, Alexandra told her of Niles's men picking her up from the abbey. She told the tale of Happy and of her reunion with Aggie. And then she told Kat about the disgusting pig her cousin had planned to marry her off to. As she described how her intended-to-be tried to examine her teeth, Kat gasped and sat up, and then gasped again at the pain she caused herself.

"What is his name?" she asked.

"Hugh Sullivan," Alexandra replied.

"No!" Kat gasped again, standing up this time. "It's the same man!" she exclaimed. "It's the same man I refused to marry! He's the reason I took this beating."

"No!" It was Alexandra's turn to gasp.

"I'd already told my father I would not marry, but he presented me to the Sullivan anyway. When he tried to check my teeth, I rammed my knee into his manhood and my fist to his throat. He went down quickly, wheezing and gagging. I guess after that he decided I wasn't wifely material. And then my father ordered this," she said and pointed to her back. "In case you haven't already guessed, my father is laird of the Campbells."

Alexandra's mouth dropped open in astonishment. This beautiful woman was nothing like the repugnant man upstairs. And she thought she'd had it rough…

"The Sullivan must have decided to try elsewhere for a wife after I ran. Our fates and our destinies seem intertwined, don't you think? We have overcome so much." She squeezed Kat's hand again, "We will get out of here."

The women slept little. They talked, and yelled and banged on their prison door throughout the night. Kat wanted to know how Alexandra had become a McGregor, so she told of helping the McGregor escape, only to find out that he was the laird and she was his prisoner. Telling of how he'd proposed, she admitted her love for him and her uncertainty of his feelings toward him, other than being physically attracted and wanting to have children.

"I would have guessed your feelings for the McGregor just by the change in the tone of your voice when you speak of him. Love... I have never experienced it, nor do I want to. No man shall own me!" Kat confessed she wished she'd been born a man. She also told Alexandra of her love for the forest and how it had become her sanctuary.

Both women were surprised by dawn's light. They'd spent the night forming a bond of friendship, and each wondered what it might have been like to have grown up with a sister.

Breakfast, which consisted of two bowls of runny porridge, was passed through the opening in the door. Alexandra jumped up to grab them and said, "Your laird is going to be very upset you didn't pass along my message sooner. For your own sake, you must get me an audience with him."

"Shut your mouth!" was the response she received from the other side of the door.

As the women ate their meager fare, they heard a raised conversation from beyond the door, but they could not make out any words. Alexandra lifted her eyebrows and looked hopefully at Kat. Maybe this would be it? The discussion soon ended and silence prevailed.

"I might be able to fit through the window," Kat said. "This dungeon was meant to hold men. If we derive a way to get me up there, I think I could fit through the bars."

"What's on the other side?" Alexandra asked.

"The courtyard. I'd have to do it during the night. Even if I get out, there's a chance I may be seen. But what do we have to lose?"

They were in the midst of discussing how they could hoist Kat up to the window when the dungeon door opened wide. Two angry looking men stood in the doorway.

"The laird will see you now," one of them said and stepped in to grab Alexandra's arm. Neither man made eye contact nor spoke to Kat. Alexandra was pulled from the room, and the door was slammed shut. She heard the rasp of the bar as it was locked. Rehearsing in her mind what she wanted to say, she was led up the steps and back into the hall. She stood once again before the laird's table, only this time, she looked upon him with contempt.

Not waiting for him to give permission to speak, she said, "I am the McGregor's wife, and I carry his child. He will stop at nothing to get me back. Your clan will be destroyed."

The room went dead silent, and then a roar erupted from the bear. Clearing the table with a sweeping motion of his arm, he sent utensils and food flying. With another roar, he picked the table up and flipped it over. Alexandra did not cringe when it landed at her feet. The man cursed violently and paced before her. Then suddenly, he stopped as if realizing she might be bluffing.

"Do you have proof?" he demanded.

Alexandra pulled up on the chain around her neck and lifted the McGregor's ring from between her breasts. She held the ring out for his inspection. The laird roughly grabbed it, bringing it, and therefore her, closer. Ignoring the sting of the chain, she stood still and watched his face when he made out the wolf head insignia. He dropped the chain as if it were hot and stepped back.

****

"We have been tricked!" he bellowed to his fellow clansmen, "Betrayed once again by a woman!" How was he going to get out of this? The reputation of the Wolf far preceded him. The kidnapping of a prize was one thing, stealing the man's wife was another. This... this the Wolf would take very seriously. He had no doubt his clan would fall in an outright war. His wealth and strength had steadily declined over the years. He had hoped this ransom business would give him the prosperity he needed to preserve the clan.

"Set me free and give me the woman, Kat, to take with me, and I will do what I can to stop a war," Alexandra said.

The old laird stopped in his tracks. Yes, that might work. He faced her and said, "Yes, tell the Wolf I was tricked! That I didn't know who you were. Tell him I give to him my only daughter as a slave and a sign of my regret."

Chapter Sixteen

When Kat was released, no one spoke or said goodbye. She rode out of the courtyard with her head held high and her face stoic, masking the mental and physical pain she had to be feeling. There were no tears. Alexandra's heart filled with sorrow and pride for her new friend.

The Campbell laird sent them on their way with supplies, and two good horses, as a gift to the McGregor. He did not send any men to escort them as he said he doubted they'd return alive, and he needed every man he had.

Alexandra had no idea which direction to take, so Kat took the lead. They galloped away from the stronghold, and as soon as they were well out of sight, they slowed their pace to a canter. It was obvious to Alexandra the horse's movements were causing her friend extreme discomfort. Pain was etched on her face, and she grimaced as the horse shifted beneath her.

"Why don't we stop so I can change your bandages?"

"We are going to be traveling in the dark as it is. I can make it," Kat said.

Alexandra nodded. She'd make sure those bandages were changed as soon as they were safe within the McGregor keep. She couldn't wait to see Ian. It seemed as if weeks had passed instead of a day and a half. What was he thinking? What was he doing? Did he think Niles was behind her kidnapping as she had, or was he on his way to the Campbell stronghold? Maybe they would cross paths. Her thoughts drifted to the babe growing within her.

****

The anticipation of getting back to Ian made the journey seem unbearably long. Darkness descended hours ago, and their progress slowed. At every clearing, Kat gazed at the stars and adjusted their direction accordingly. Alexandra had full confidence in her abilities, but as the day progressed, she watched the strength drain from the woman. Alexandra prayed Kat would stay conscious. Surely the McGregor stronghold was not much farther.

Finally, Alexandra saw the moonlight reflect off the lake by the keep. They were on the opposite side and would have to ride around it, but at least she knew where they were.

"We're here!" she exclaimed, "I can lead the way. It's just beyond the lake."

Kat's shoulders and head dropped at the news. "Thank God," she said, and slumped even farther over the horse until her head rested alongside its mane.

As the women approached the keep, Alexandra noticed the gate to the village wall was closed. She continuously called out as she got closer, "It is I, Alexandra." It would be a real shame to get shot by her own clan after all she'd been through. When she was right in front of the gate and she could be clearly seen, the gate opened and they entered. Immediately, a group of warriors surrounded them. Her eyes scanned over them looking for the McGregor. Where was he? She thought she saw him parting the gathering crowd, but as the figure drew closer she saw it was James.

"Welcome home," James said and helped her to dismount, "We have much to discuss." James's attention turned to Kat still slumped over her horse.

"I should have guessed the Campbells had something to do with this," he said with contempt in his voice and grabbed Kat's arm before Alexandra could stop him.

Kat awoke instantly on guard. Alexandra watched in horror as Kat kicked James hard under his jaw-line, snapping his head back. They all watched as he fell backward to the ground like a cut tree.

Several things happened at once. Clan members drew weapons and pushed forward. Alexandra screamed, "No. No. No! Don't hurt her!" She lifted her arms high and threw herself in front of Kat.

"Her?" James yelled, "What the...?" He rose to his feet rubbing his jaw and moving it side to side. He glared at Kat and she glared back at him. Several people stifled chuckles until someone yelled out, "It's not often you're bested by a man, let alone a wisp of a woman," and then the rest of the crowd joined in the laughter.

"Please. She's my friend and she's hurt. We need to get her inside," Alexandra explained as Kat slid from her horse. "Where's Ian?"

"We'll talk as soon as you get *her* settled," James replied.

****

Alexandra took Kat's hand and pulled her into the keep's main hall where more clan members, mostly women, surrounded and greeted her. Debra was one of the first to step forward.

"I had no idea an ambush was waiting for us. Poor Robert is dead," Debra sniffled.

"I'm so sorry for your loss," Alexandra squeezed her hand, noting the woman's battered face.

Maddie rushed forward and gave her a hug. "Thank God you are okay. We were so worried."

"I'm fine. I just need to see to my new friend's wounds. Can you please bring some hot soapy water and fresh bandages? I will introduce you all to her later," Alexandra said and pushed her way through the gathered women. She led Kat to her and Ian's bedchamber and had her lie down while they waited for Maddie.

"Who was the red-haired woman with the bruised face?" Kat asked.

"Debra McCaw. I was at her home when I was abducted."

"You were betrayed by a red-haired woman. I did not see her. I only heard about her later. She came to my laird with a plan for us to kidnap and ransom you. There's something about this woman—" Kat stopped when Maddie entered the room with supplies.

Alexandra instructed the girl to soak Kat's bindings with hot soapy water before removing them. She quickly mixed together the healing paste and told Maddie how to apply it.

"I am sorry to leave you, but you are in good hands. I must find out what's happened to the McGregor. We will talk more when I return," she said anxiously, bending to give Kat's hand a reassuring squeeze.

"Go," Kat mumbled into the pillow, already fading

into sleep.

Alexandra knew Kat wouldn't be sleeping for long, once those bandages were removed, but she hoped the pain would be more tolerable this time. Hurrying down the steps, she saw James watching and waiting from their usual table. The hall was deserted other than for a few servants cleaning up.

"Ian?" she asked and slid into the chair across from him.

"He has taken most of our warriors, and he's headed after Niles."

"But it was the Campbell who took me."

"We found evidence of a Sullivan tartan at Robert's cabin, and we followed a trail leading south toward Niles. Ian and our warriors left this morning at dawn. He instructed me to stay behind to defend our home in case Niles and Sullivan have set a trap. One of Ian's couriers arrived back here at dusk with news. Scouts sent ahead reported back that Niles and a large army are on the move, headed north toward us. My men and I will leave at daybreak to join Ian.

Alexandra was so confused. She covered her face with her hands and said, "This is like a chess game I can't comprehend!"

The only thing she clearly understood was that Ian was in danger. Fear grabbed and squeezed her heart. She couldn't breathe and the room started to spin. Putting her head between her legs, she tried to keep from passing out.

James knelt by her and put his hand over her trembling shoulder. "There is no better leader than the Wolf. Our men are each worth ten of theirs. This will all be over soon," he said with confidence. There was no worry in his voice.

"I do need to hear how the Campbells are involved," he said and moved back to his seat.

She took several more breaths and lifted her head to detail everything she remembered about her abduction and what she'd seen or heard at the Campbell stronghold. When she spoke of learning Kat was the Campbell laird's daughter and of how terribly the woman had been treated, James said nothing, but she saw his eyes harden. She didn't know if it was because he was still angry at being kicked or if it was due to Kat's treatment at the hand of her father.

After answering all his questions, Alexandra went to check on Kat, and James left to get a few hours' sleep before he had to set out in the morning with his warriors.

Maddie had just finished changing Kat's bandages and was cleaning up when Alexandra returned. Kat was awake and lying on her stomach, but she was not crying. The strength and self-control of this woman simply amazed Alexandra. She thanked Maddie for her help and arranged for a permanent room to be prepared in the morning for her new friend.

Alexandra sat down on the bed next to Kat. "Back to Debra, you think she is involved somehow?"

"There is something about her demeanor I don't trust. Warning prickles crawled down my spine as she talked to you. I know that sounds silly, but I've grown use to observing people since I'm usually left out and avoided. I've learned to trust my instincts. I'm not saying she did it, but she bears watching."

"We did get off to a poor start. She sent me some hateful looks, but I'd thought we moved past that and were heading toward friendship. And there are many red-headed women here, including Maddie who I adore."

"I didn't mean to upset you," Kat said, "Just watch your back around her, okay?"

"I will. Try to get some rest now." Alexandra smothered the candle. "I have too many thoughts chasing around in my head to sleep." She curled up in the chair next to the window and looked out into the darkness. She spent the night pleading with God for her husband's safe return.

In the pre-dawn light, she watched from the window as the men gathered below. The sound of warriors and horses woke Kat, and she stirred and propped herself up. "Have you been up all night?"

"Most of it. I nodded off several times. I hate this waiting and worrying. What if I never see him again? What if he never knows about the babe I carry? Surely, God will have mercy?" Her eyes teared up before she added with building anger, "Is this a woman's lot in life? To wait for news of life or death? To do nothing to help the man she loves, but sit and pray?"

"Does your God not allow action?"

Alexandra looked at her puzzled.

Throwing back blankets, Kat slowly sat up and simply said, "Let's follow."

Alexandra stared at her in astonishment.

Kat shrugged and started to dress. "Why not? No man rules me. I doubt if they'd let us join them, but they can't keep us from following."

"Are you sure you're well enough?" Alexandra asked, holding back hope, "I know I should not let you, but I wholeheartedly want to go."

Kat smiled, "I don't want to miss this myself."

They dressed and gathered supplies while they waited for the men to leave. Alexandra grabbed her bow and handed Kat her dagger.

Kat wryly stared at the small blade and said, "It's better than nothing, I suppose. My own weapons were not returned to me."

The women watched from the window and waited until the warriors left before heading to the stables. Readying the horses they'd ridden the night before, they were soon on the trail. It wasn't hard to follow and Alexandra probably could have tracked it herself, but she was very glad to have Kat by her side.

For the rest of the day, they pushed their horses, stopping only to rest and water them as needed. By late evening, the McGregor warriors finally stopped and set up camp. The women slept rolled in blankets on the ground within sight of the warriors' campfires. Alexandra was exhausted from all the riding and the stress of the last few days. She did not expect to get much sleep on the hard, cold ground. Surprisingly, once her eyes closed, she remembered nothing until Kat shook her awake before dawn to tell her the warriors were already on the move.

By midafternoon the next day, James and his men caught up with the rest of the McGregor fighters, but they didn't stay long. James's group pushed on under cover of the forest. Perhaps, she wondered, to attack from the rear?

Kat stopped and positioned them on a ridge with the forest at their backs and a clear view of the valley and meadow before them. The McGregor warriors were spread out at the north end and faced off against Niles and Sullivan to the south. Alexandra easily recognized the McGregor, riding back and forth on his black stallion in front of his men. She heard his voice yelling instructions, but the wind carried his words away before they reached her. He bent to accept a white flag from one of his men, and galloped alone to the center of the meadow between the two armies.

"What is he doing?" Alexandra anxiously looked at Kat.

"It looks like he is asking for a parlay. He wants to talk to the other leaders."

As Alexandra watched, she saw Niles, accompanied by guards, trotting out on their horses to face the McGregor.

****

Niles was extremely disappointed he had not been able to ambush the McGregor clan with a surprise advance on them. Who had tipped them off? Oh well, he obviously had three times as many men as the McGregor. It should be a simple enough victory, and then he'd bring back that bitch, Alexandra. He wished he could make sure she died in his attempted 'rescue,' but she was worth far too much money. Better to let the Sullivan kill her slowly, he thought and smiled.

The McGregor unexpectedly took the field, and Niles was curious as to what he had to say. Perhaps so outnumbered, the man was willing to concede victory and offer compensation. Niles ordered his inner guard to accompany him. With anticipation, he rode out to meet the McGregor.

"Give me Alexandra," the McGregor demanded, "and you can take me as prisoner in her place."

Niles was taken aback, both by the intimidating

stature of the large man up close on his beast of a horse, and by the words that came out of the man's mouth. Careful to conceal his astonishment, he quickly calculated his options. *He thinks I have her! Where is Alexandra?*

"Alexandra is my ward. It is my duty to protect her," he answered smugly.

"She is my wife!" the McGregor shouted, eyes flashing, "So she is of no use to you now."

Niles was speechless. The possibility hadn't occurred to him. Furious at being outwitted, he stalled several moments to consider his choices before he accepted the offer.

"Send Alexandra over first," the McGregor ordered.

"No," Niles said coldly.

The McGregor started to dismount when both men spotted movement on the ridge. A horse and rider charged down it straight between the two armies. The rider was small. Gold hair billowed like a flag behind her.

****

Alexandra saw the McGregor draw his sword while Niles's inner guard surrounded him and attacked from all sides. *Please God, protect him!* She crouched low over her horse's mane and urged him to fly. Niles maneuvered his horse behind the McGregor and lifted his sword over his head with both hands, ready to plunge it into the McGregor's back.

With no time to spare, she charged her horse into Niles's steed. The two horses collided and time slowed. Piercing sounds of her screams combined with the horses' high-pitched squeals as horses and riders rolled in a ball of horseflesh and hooves.

Alexandra felt herself sailing through the air and instinctively tucked her head. A hoof skimmed her cheek, and she landed with a teeth-jarring thud onto her back. She couldn't breathe. Was the McGregor okay? Where was Niles? She started to panic and willed air back into her lungs so she could move.

Niles's face loomed above hers, and she struggled to rise. He knocked her back down and straddled her. Blood dripped from a wound on his forehead. He snarled and gripped her throat in his hands. With eyes wide with hate, he cursed her. Spittle dropped in her face as he squeezed her throat. She clawed at his hands but she couldn't loosen his grip or pry his fingers away. She went for his eyes, but his arms were too long and he pulled his head out of reach. Her vision started to fade. She feared she was going to die...*But did the McGregor live?*

Suddenly, Niles was gone. Or at least his head was. Was she seeing things? She rasped in air as his headless body dropped to her side. The McGregor's frowning face appeared over hers, and she felt herself lifted to her feet. Tears of relief streamed down her face, and she grabbed him tightly. She never wanted to let him go.

They stood holding each other, ignoring the wave of clan warriors who ran around and past, screaming blood-curdling war cries. The moment the McGregor had pulled his sword, his warriors had charged toward their foes. Having witnessed their leader's beheading, the enemy fought only moments before retreating straight into James's army.

"Thank God, you are okay," Ian said in her ear, before kissing her. Holding her face in his hands, he asked, "Woman, you scared the life out of me. When are you going to start staying out of danger?"

She looked up into his dark eyes and her words tumbled out hoarsely. "I had to see you. I had to tell you that I love you. What if something had happened and I never got to speak those words?" Tears of joy ran down her face. She was so happy he was alive. "I am so sorry for all the trouble I've caused you."

"Aye, you are trouble! I didn't want to give you my heart, but you have stolen it from me. It's because of *who* you are that I love you. You are a most courageous woman, one who risks her life for others. A laird could not ask for a better wife. I am proud of you, and I wouldn't want you to be any other way," he said and kissed her again.

It took a moment for his words to sink in. He was saying he loved her! He really loved her! Tears began flowing in earnest now, and she couldn't control them. She laughed at herself for laughing and crying at the same time. The McGregor laughed with her and grabbed her around the waist to lift her high in the air, only to release and catch her, pulling her close for a long, passionate kiss.

Epilogue

Alexandra leaned back against the fluffed-up pillows. She was beyond exhaustion and yet, at the same time, she'd never been so excited. Her eyes watched Kat clean her newborn son and swaddle him before she returned to Alexandra's bedside and gently placed him in her arms.

"He's beautiful," Kat said.

"Aye, like his father. I can't take my eyes off of him," Alexandra said with a tired laugh.

Staring at the child in the crook of her arm, Alexandra wondered if she was dreaming. He was just as she imagined he would be. Fingering his tiny hand, she admired his thick dark hair and his large brown eyes.

Suddenly, without warning, the bedchamber door crashed open. It slammed against the wall only to swing back again toward the McGregor who froze in the doorway. Startled, Alexandra looked up in time to see the fleeting emotions that crossed his face as he entered the room and rushed to her side. Panic, relief, love, and awe. He knelt and engulfed her, placing one arm on the pillow over her head and the other around her arms holding the baby.

Kat slipped out unnoticed and closed the door behind her.

"I came as soon as I could. The unexpected snow

slowed us down considerably." Ian kissed her and asked, "All went well? You are okay? The babe?"

"Yes, meet your son." Alexandra tenderly transferred her son into her husband's arms. Her heart was so full of love, it could burst.

Ian stood and held the babe out in front of him. Staring at the child with amazement, he declared proudly, "I told you we would have a son."

"Aye, and I told you we'd have a daughter," Alexandra smiled as she answered.

As if on cue, a tiny cry emerged from the crib that stood against the wall. Ian looked toward the crib and then down at the babe in his hands and back at the crib once more.

Alexandra laughed at the incredulous look on his face. She held up her arms to take her son and said, "Why don't you go say hello to your daughter?"

A word from the author...

I live in a small Midwestern town with three critters, my husband, a cat, and a dog. I love reading, writing, and family game nights.